THE
THING
IN THE
WIND

BILL MULLEN

Let the world know:
#IGotMyCLPBook!

Crystal Lake Publishing
www.CrystalLakePub.com

**Follow us on
Amazon:**

WELCOME
TO ANOTHER

CRYSTAL LAKE PUBLISHING
CREATION

Join today at www.crystallakepub.com & www.patreon.com/CLP

For David

"Great revelations of nature, of course, never fail to impress in one way or another, and I was no stranger to moods of the kind. Mountains overawe and oceans terrify, while the mystery of great forests exercises a spell peculiarly its own. But all these, at one point or another, somewhere link on intimately with human life and human experience. They stir comprehensible, even if alarming, emotions. They tend on the whole to exalt."

—Algernon Blackwood

PROLOGUE:
MAX THE BOY

THE WORD CAME from a far-off place where wind is born. It woke the boy. Moonlight glowed through his lone window as shadows of gale-blown hemlock and juniper danced on the floor like deranged demons clawing their way past the veil on a Samhain night. Vision blurry with sleep dust, he glanced at indistinct shapes until locking on to the black sliver between the jamb and closet door. He shivered. Something was in there. Staring back at him with black eyes and malicious intent. The devil's eyes. But he'd been taught that the devil was male. The sound that had woken him wasn't like any male he'd ever heard. No male had a voice that seductive and full of sorrow; it sounded like an echo, hollow and distant. Not from the closet or under the bed. He wiped the rheum from his eyes, then gazed at the window. The sound was beyond the log walls of the winter-lashed cabin and hidden somewhere out in that coniferous maze flailing wildly under a full moon.

Lured out of bed with uncontrollable curiosity, the boy left his fear in the damp sheets and crept out of his tenebrous room, tiptoed down the hallway to the living room, where a sluggish fire glowed, and he eyed his skinny doppelganger in the front door window. The warped pane reflected more like mercury than a mirror, showing not a healthy adolescent, but a disfigured sideshow exhibit, pale skin glowing red as if sunburned. He stared at his hideous reflection with odd fascination: his left eye and cheek blending with his forehead, his other eye low near his mouth. He swayed, his shirtless body twisting and dipping and expanding with the slightest motion, how it dimmed and brightened and

1

changed hue in tune with the fire's mood, surreal art in the flesh. If he turned a certain way, he didn't have arms, in another way no legs. And yet another showed him with two forearms grown out of one elbow, yet no feet. Then, he saw the fire burning in his lopsided blue eyes. Unnatural. Feral. He shuddered. The game wasn't fun anymore.

"*Max.*"

The wind-washed words broke his concentration. Fear had found him again, knees trembling. He grabbed the side of the sofa to balance himself. His eyes darted frantically from item to item in the room: table, door, reflection, recliner, fire, until they settled on another pair of eyes, these dark and lifeless. He knew the sound couldn't be coming from the moose head above the fireplace, but the animal's gaze stopped him and seized his attention. For a moment, he felt sorrow for the animal and, to his surprise, felt the sudden urge to weep. Before the lump was able to form in his throat, the fire popped and threw his sights back on the front door and his grotesque image in the warped pane. By some strange mesmeric force he couldn't explain, the boy unlocked the front door and eased outside shirtless and shoeless into shin-deep snow. Icy wind smacked his bare sweaty flesh, making his muscles tense, but his mind ignored the stinging cold as he trudged toward the blustery forest.

"*Max.*"

His walk became a jog between tall pines, each rubbery sound of mashed snow underfoot taking him one step closer to the eerie, crying voice, and one step farther from his warm home. Branches overhead groaned and cast craggy shadows along the undisturbed, snowy ground in front of him, but they didn't slow him down. Almost unconsciously, he zigzagged through the trees, gaining more speed. After nearly a minute of adrenaline-charged pursuit, the boy finally felt the cold, and his sight blurred for a moment. He slowed down as frigid wind hacked its way down his throat. His body heavy as if packed with ice, he hunched over and put his hands on his knees, raggedly sucking in as much air as his frosted lungs could handle. His head throbbed, but his vision improved. Glancing around, he realized that he'd made it to a glade or the top of a frozen lake. At the farthest end, a great moose stood at the tree line, its palmate antlers the largest he'd ever seen. But it wasn't the antlers that stole his gaze, it was the animal's fiery eyes veiled behind white puffs of its exhaled breath. His own breath clouded part of his sight, or maybe it was just the blurriness coming back. His mouth fell open and he mashed his eyelids closed. The cold had made him dizzy, and the darkness his closed eyelids afforded him was the only comfort. "It isn't real," he said to himself.

In a shrill cry, the voice replied, "*Max!*"

When he flung his lids open, he thought he saw the moose explode into a million snowflakes and charge after him in the midst of a whistling gale that flung his black hair back and made him instinctively wrap his thin arms around himself and scream as loud as his frosted voice box allowed, but the wind's howl swallowed his cry. In seconds, the gale had circled the glade and had passed. But behind it came another! Heavier. Sharper. Icier. He closed his eyes again and he tightened his grip around his torso. When would it end?

The wind shrieked. It intensified. "*Max!*"

His heart felt like a jagged chunk of thumping ice. Then, as if the air grew hands, it gripped the boy's body. His eyes blew open in terror. It wasn't just wind! It couldn't be! He tried to scream again, but had no air. He couldn't move. Without warning, the freezing grip tightened, and the boy saw his bare legs leap out of the snow at lightning speed.

CHAPTER 1:
SHIRLEY CARSON WELLS

i

THREE DAYS AFTER Shirley Carson Wells was born, her drunk father slapped her mother Penny for the first time. The first time Penny hit him back was about a minute later. She picked up the heavy Holy Bible from her nightstand and slammed the spine of the book against Gary's head, connecting just under the temple. It knocked his two hundred pounds down to the dirty wooden floor of their home. Gary didn't fight back. He only lay there gazing up at her for what felt like an hour before closing his eyes and falling asleep. The time was 11:30 p.m. The date, October 30, 1966. The thought of taking little Shirley and leaving crossed Penny's mind for a moment before she just shook her head and hoped it would be the last time such a thing would happen. Shirley had been asleep when this violence occurred, but she'd read about it fifteen years later after discovering her mother's journals while trashing her parents' bedroom.

Penny Wells hadn't read much outside of the Holy Bible, but something had snagged her attention one Sunday during her junior year of high school—just two years prior to getting married—while walking with her parents to a restaurant after church. They'd passed Prescott Books, a tiny bookstore that had opened recently in Whittle Springs, a small neighborhood in Knoxville, Tennessee. The cover was simple, but the title intriguing—*Silent Spring* by Rachel Carson. It was a used copy but in new condition, and the following day, after school, she marched into Prescott Books and bought the copy with some of the money she'd saved from babysitting the neighbor's sullen children. The shop owner, a hippie woman from San Francisco named Shirley Laurence, slipped a small journal into her bag and touched Penny's hand.

"Enjoy the book, dear," Shirley said. "It's probably the most important book of our time." Handing Penny the bag, she added, "And use the journal—my little gift to you—to reflect. Because we can't just read words, we have to ingest them and do something with them."

And Penny did. She soaked up every word Carson wrote, jotted down her thoughts on her journal's pages, and began to change, to care about what was going on around her, and to start using terms like organophosphorus, chlorinated hydrocarbon, and phosphates. She'd go back to Prescott Books and have long conversations with Shirley about the environment, about the conflict in Vietnam, and about a myriad of other topics she felt she couldn't talk about *out there in the real world*. She started hating neighbors who'd spray poison on weeds or anthills, and she brought up the issues with using DDT and other poisons in her biology class, but she was often overlooked and ignored by Mr. Hess, who also attended her church. While Jesus might have filled her spiritual self, the environment filled everything else. It was Carson's book that raised awareness, that caused people to start caring a bit more, that caused Penny to start thinking differently, but it didn't last long. Some classmates started making fun of her, giving her the nickname Penny Dreadful because, as Avery Lauder had put it, "Every time she opens her mouth, she has something bad to say, and I just dread it, man. I fuckin' dread it."

And then her pastor, Phillip-Lee Youngblood, talked to her and her parents a few months later after church service about the destructive behavior Penny had been displaying. "'Let a woman learn in silence with all submission. And I do not permit a woman to teach or to have authority over a man, but to be in silence'." He said that it wasn't Christian for a young girl to journey down the path of activism, that she needed to stay on the path of the Lord. If there was a message she wanted to spread, then they had missionary work and she could "'Go into all the world and preach the gospel to every creature . . . In My name they will cast out demons; they will speak with new tongues; they will take up serpents; and if they drink anything deadly it will by no means hurt them; they will lay hands on the sick, and they will recover'."

After the discussion (well, not discussion . . . more like a monologue filled with quotes that mostly chastised her), Penny declined the missionary work and told Pastor Youngblood and her parents that she was sorry and would do what God wanted her to do. She kept her mouth shut at school, especially in her science classes (she knew Mr. Hess had been whispering to the pastor), feeling like they were all spying on her, treating her like she was a communist or something. Though they quickly became satisfied because she kept it all inside, hidden. It stayed there, growing inside her. And shortly after she had turned eighteen, she married Gary Wells, a good Christian boy that lived over on Maxwell Street and whose parents were close friends with Penny's mother and father. It seemed like the final element to appease her parents and pastor, so she went along with it. Penny was pregnant three months later. And when her daughter was born, she named her Shirley, after the bookstore owner, the woman who had accepted and guided her toward her true desire and passion, who hadn't judged her. And she had given her the middle name Carson, for Rachel, the woman whose writing had opened her eyes and had given her true desire for *her* kind to reach the greater good . . . far more than anything she'd read in the Holy Bible or that had come out of Pastor Youngblood's mouth on a Sunday morning. Her worldview, her desires and dreams, and her passions, they were all sealed up in her mind . . . and her journals.

Gary had stopped attending church once Penny had gotten pregnant, choosing to read and interpret the holy book on his own and quote convenient and out-of-context passages when he needed to manipulate Penny and bend her to his will. Through the nine months and two weeks of the pregnancy, he had steadily upped his intake of Jack Daniels from one drink per night to half a bottle. He said that it would be the last drink he'd take after the night he'd hit Penny the first time, and the book that he'd tried to interpret on his own came crashing below his temple.

According to the journals, however, Shirley calculated that it went on to happen once a month, and she saw it firsthand just before she became a teenager. Although horrified, she kept it to herself.

Gary was tall and thin, a dark beard covering his acne scars, and deep-set brown eyes that never seemed to exist without dark half-moons underneath. He'd had several jobs in those fifteen years, starting with landscaping, then railroad work, and had finally taken a position at the Knoxville Zoo, which, after many ups and downs, had finally gotten proper funding and attendance to get it modernized and secure by 1972. He'd worked there taking care of the grounds, then would come home to drink the local spirits and smoke and preach and argue until he passed out, only to wake and do it all over again the next day. He died in 1987 from liver cancer, specifically hepatocellular carcinoma. Penny lasted a few more years until succumbing to carbon monoxide poisoning from a leaky gas line to the stove. Shirley hadn't attended either funeral.

When Shirley had turned fifteen amid the increasing violence in her home, a young sophomore at Fulton High School, something changed inside her. It started when her parents had gone to Gatlinburg for the weekend, and Shirley's curiosity had gotten the best of her. She had grown resentful of her father for his drinking and for his violence toward her mother, but she admired her mother, a mere bantamweight, for always fighting back. Somehow, it seemed to make the fights much shorter than they would have been. However, it left her mother quiet most of the time. Shirley had rarely had a conversation with the woman, but it was what she yearned for as she began coming of age. So, when her parents were gone that weekend, only one week into the school year, that *something inside her* pulled her out through the front door of their brick ranch-style house and to the sidewalk. She looked to her right toward Valley View Baptist Church, then left toward Christ the Rock. If she gazed forward and could see beyond the houses no more than a hundred yards, she'd find Foster Chapel Baptist Church. She was surrounded by God, by Jesus, by churchgoers and holy people, but, within the confines of her home, she was in Hell. Her mother would tell her robotically "'that older women . . . admonish the young women to love their husbands, to love their children, to be discreet, chaste, homemakers, good, obedient to their own husbands, that the word of God may not be blasphemed'" and to "'obey your parents in the Lord, for this is right. Honor your father and mother, which is the first commandment with promise . . . '" That she and Shirley must attend church every Sunday morning and Wednesday night and repent for any wrongdoing. Penny would insist this with such fervor that Shirley suspected her mother's mind to be full of devilish and vengeful thoughts because, aside from defending herself, the woman did nothing wrong. Her father would say the prayer just before dinner each night, quote select scripture like "Wives, submit to your own husbands, as to the Lord. For the husband is the head of the wife" and "Your desire shall be for your husband, and he shall rule over you" when he felt that Penny had started talking about something he didn't want her talking about while they sat trying to have a family discussion, and then he let the devil slip inside him after his last bite of dinner and first sip of Jack.

These distant and recent memories built up inside her like water and steam inside a geyser, her eruption a tear-filled scream that bellowed out there to the neighborhood: "Hypocrites!" But there was no one outside to hear. More importantly, it wasn't for others to hear. It was her metamorphosis, her peeling back the veil, her exiting the cocoon whose comforting and moral qualities had turned to poison.

She'd heard stories about the pastor. She knew of terrible deeds and gossip among the congregation. She'd been to friends' houses and witnessed blasphemy and sin with every flap of each person's tongue. It was all bullshit! And it hit her hard . . . so hard that she wanted to fall to her knees right there on that sidewalk and weep. But, she remained strong. She turned around, wiped her eyes, and saw clearly for the first time as she made her way slowly back inside. What sparked the rebellion and the need to tear apart her parents' room had always remained a mystery to her. She opened the small closet and threw all the clothes onto the floor. On the closet shelf were three boxes that she pulled down, opened, and tore through. Nothing of interest. Trophies and plaques from her father's basketball playing days in high school. Yearbooks. Stacks of photos that she didn't care about. Paperwork. Two bibles. Several crucifixes and other church items. One box was full of wedding junk that they had probably forgotten about. It all ended up in piles on the floor.

Exhausted, Shirley lay back on the green shag carpet feeling defeated. That undefined urge to find something had only led her to creating a mess. When she exhaled a deep breath, her gaze shifted from the ceiling to the bed, that line of shadow between the bed skirt and carpet seeming to tug at her. Rolling onto her side, she reached out and lifted the bed skirt, the sunlight revealing something under her mother's side. Inching closer, Shirley thrust her arm under the bed, the skirt falling and causing her to search blindly for whatever was hidden back there. Then she felt it. Not it

THE THING IN THE WIND

. . . them. A small stack of notebooks, the kind she used in high school. There were six of them, and she pulled them out into the light. Each had a year printed on the cover: 1981, 1980, 1979, 1978, 1977, and 1976. There had to be more, so she lifted the bed skirt again and flattened her body on the floor. A slight musty odor filled her sinuses followed by a visible cloud of dust that made her sneeze and her eyes water. It made her think of an old person's room that hadn't been vacuumed in years. After wiping her eyes, she noticed more stacks of notebooks pushed midway where the light barely reached. With just a hint of straining, Shirley reached them with her fingertips, grabbed for them, and after inching them toward her the first three tries, finally gripped the bottom of the first stack and pulled them to her. When she'd made sure all of them were out from under the bed, she saw that they went all the way back to 1963. And there was a dusty first edition of Rachel Carson's *Silent Spring*, several pages dogeared, next to the last stack as well. She gathered them all together greedily like a pirate does his booty and took them to her bedroom.

Shirley began reading the notebooks. As the sun dropped down behind the Smoky Mountains, she stayed awake, reading and reading some more. She learned about her mother, about how she'd started down the path of independence, the path of free thinking, the path she wanted to go down, and how the neighborhood, the pastor, her church, her parents, and even her own teacher—weren't teachers supposed to support this sort of thinking?—stood in her way and blocked her in. Penny had faltered and fallen into what they demanded of her. How Shirley wished Prescott Books was still open and the owner, Shirley, was still there so she could venture in and talk about anything. How she could ask what kind of person her mother used to be. There was still a spark, but it was dulled by conformity. It gave Shirley an immense feeling of sadness, but she didn't let it stop her from reading on. And she did so until noon on Sunday. She realized that she'd missed church and vowed to never attend again. Not feeling exhausted after nearly twenty-seven hours of reading, Shirley put the notebooks back under the bed and knew that she'd have to give it time to sink in, all those years of experiences, intimate thoughts, regrets . . . oh, the regrets. However, for her, the breach of privacy would never be a regret because she knew truths that would not, could not, have been passed on to her. She was smart enough to

9

know how flawed memories could be, smart enough to know that those journals were as close to reality as possible. Now she really knew her mother and knew what parts seemed to have been passed on to her. She finally knew all the things that her mother had wanted to say to her, how her mother had wanted to raise her, and how much pain she had been in until, as far as Shirley could interpret, she had let most of herself die . . . the only bit of life remaining in her fighting back when Gary got violent.

Leaving the mess of the closet contents on the floor and taking *Silent Spring* with her, Shirley pushed open the back door, walked through the backyard, and kicked open the fence door that separated their property from the forest behind their home. She'd never wandered into that dark forest in all of her fifteen years. There was something about its mystery that kept her away, something about how the mist always seemed to linger there longer than anywhere else. It reminded her of the forest Young Goodman Brown ventured into, that Nathaniel Hawthorne short story she'd read in her freshman English course last year. He'd gone into the forest, met the devil, lost his faith . . . lost his Faith, and it damaged him forevermore. Sure, it could have all been a nightmare full of witches and a black mass, a nightmare that was so profound it caused his life to change, but those kinds of things didn't give her fear and dread . . . It was the idea that everything you thought to be true suddenly becomes false, that all of your friends are your enemies, that all of your morals and virtues are immoral and flawed, and that the person you've chosen to take life's journey with turns out to be untrustworthy, secretive, and in league with all those things that you oppose while keeping you oblivious with surface-level niceties. No one wants to have to question everything, to scrutinize every detail while searching for some grain of truth. No. They want to know and trust that they've chosen a good person, a person who has their best interests at heart. Was that something that had happened to her mother? Had Penny been beguiled by Gary? Was he really some sort of demon, some incubus sucking away all her energy and will? As Shirley blew past the gate, she didn't care anymore. Her father was a tyrant, her mother beaten down and brainwashed, both slaves to the Baptist ministry in their own way. She would have none of it anymore. Into the forest, no worries, no dread. She would not give in like she felt her mother had. She would return enlightened like Young Goodman

THE THING IN THE WIND

Brown, and damn any consequences that might await her upon that return.

The Tennessee heat bore down on her until she reached the shade of the trees—a mixture of pine, oak, walnut, and several others that she couldn't identify. It didn't take long to find a comfortable nook among an oak tree surrounded by a tightly knit group of pine trees, the acidic needles coating the ground and preventing anything from growing. While it wasn't quite the perfect circle, the pines surrounded her and her oak almost as if by design, like some natural place of worship. As she sat against the large trunk, Shirley felt a warm and tingly wave pass through her body, as if the oak had shared some of its deep-rooted energy with her, as if it had welcomed her to read to her captivated audience. And she accepted, taking in a deep breath and opening the book. The spine of the tome creaked and cracked like something out of a horror film, but it didn't dissuade her. Past the publication information and table of contents, Shirley read . . . *A Fable for Tomorrow* . . .

ii

A sliver of ivory moon lingered in the sky as Shirley returned from the woods. She spied her parents through the back windows, and they didn't seem worried, just angry. Gary, with his hands on his hips and pointing toward the bedroom. Penny sitting and listening. But neither said anything to her as she charged inside, slung open the refrigerator door, grabbed a soda, and disappeared into her bedroom. She had gotten through half the book out there in the woods. Exhaustion hit suddenly, so she'd made her way back home. When Shirley stood next to her mattress, her body lost all its strength to stay upright. With the overhead light still burning, she collapsed onto the bed, legs off the side of the mattress, and fell into a deep sleep, the cold can of Pepsi beginning to sweat in her hand.

Screaming woke her . . . her own screaming! She'd never had such a vivid nightmare before. Her skin was gooseflesh, her chest like a vise. Shirley was so cold, but the room was so warm and humid. She sat up, her damp clothes clinging to her skin. Gathering her wits, she breathed in deeply and out again several times until her heartbeat eased and her body temperature was back to normal.

11

She felt the rebellious spirit of her mother within her and knew that she would have to take the reins and run with it, beginning with her words. Shirley ripped a piece of paper out of her science notebook and wrote all the details of her dream that she could remember—a cabin, a moose head above a fireplace, going out into a snowstorm, running, and then . . . what? How did it end? She couldn't remember . . .

iii

At school that day, Shirley wondered if the teachers would react similarly to the new Shirley as they had her mother nearly two decades ago. Not only had she changed over that rebellious weekend, but, unlike her mother, she refused to retreat even one step. It didn't take long to learn that her demeanor was not welcome by most, but the shifts and waves the country had been embracing left her with a safety net of classmates that welcomed a free thinker. One among the group was her crush from gym class— Richard Simpson. He had been tall and lanky during freshman year, thick braces keeping him from smiling much, and his brown hair often looked unwashed with specks of dandruff sprinkled where his hair parted down the center of his head. But just before sophomore year had begun, the braces came off, and he began to understand the importance of good personal hygiene. He'd grown into his height so that he wasn't so lanky anymore, a growth spurt that allowed his body to fit into his much more fashionable older brother's hand-me-downs. So, with a rush of confidence, the trait that was most attractive to Shirley, he grabbed her attention, along with several other girls', even juniors. Rather than continuing to keep her feelings inside and letting her mind run wild with desirable scenarios, she simply approached him that Monday in the hallway while he was rummaging through his locker and tried out the new Shirley.

"I have a crush on you, Richard Simpson," she said. "I want to know what your lips feel like against mine."

Richard froze for a moment, then he looked at her, a cocky smile spreading across his face. He smiled much more often now that his braces were off and his teeth straight. "That can happen anytime you'd like."

Even though he attended church as often as her mother, he was also miles from perfect. And, so, the following evening, they met in those devilish woods, made out, and ended up making love for nearly three unremarkable sticky minutes. When it was over, the crush that she'd had simply disappeared like finding out the answer to a benign riddle . . . "I have towns but no houses, forests but no trees, rivers but no fish . . . " Once figured out, "okay," and then you move on, "Hardly aware of her departed lover; Her brain allows one half-formed thought to pass: 'Well now that's done: and I'm glad it's over'."

The following day, Shirley made it clear that they were not a pair, not a couple, and that, as long as he was okay with that, they could go for "hikes" in the woods behind her house whenever they wanted to, with the hope that it would get better each time. It was those words that made Richard fall in love with her that year in high school. She let this happen, figuring that it was easier to let him imagine she was interested in him for more than hikes. Besides, he did what she needed him to do, all the things a good Southern boyfriend should do—open doors, carry her books, hold her hand, take her to dances, take her on dates at one of the nearby cheap restaurants. She never said that she loved him or made herself vulnerable emotionally, keeping enough distance so that he wouldn't have too much pain when she moved on. And the occasional lovemaking, the "hiking," did get better, but it wasn't something that Shirley craved, and certainly not something that seemed so sinful as her former pastor consistently spouted from his pulpit every chance he had to get people to conform: "Marriage is honorable among all, and the bed undefiled; but fornicators and adulterers God will judge."

Shirley wasn't surprised when neither of her parents seemed to notice that she would venture into the woods alone most afternoons when school let out or for long periods of time on weekend days. When she was alone and surrounded by those trees, she never had a supernatural experience, never felt anything but energy around her, natural energy. Earth was alive, and she felt thankful to be allowed to exist upon its flesh, to admire the trees, which she imagined to be strands of its hair. Would that make her nothing more than a louse, scurrying through the hair and dandruff of a being so much larger and sophisticated than her own? Some parasite feeding off its host, not giving it anything in return, just taking and taking and taking some more? Yes, that was it. That was the revelation that came to her about a month after losing her virginity, a few weeks after finishing *Silent Spring*. Humans were parasites feeding off the earth. Jesus Christ! Was she to be one of those ultra-left-wing environmental extremists? That's what she had felt like when this epiphany ignited in her mind, but she dismissed it quickly, knowing that she just had a deep understanding of the human role in it all, that a single human on Earth was insignificant, that a single human in the grand scheme of the universe was more insignificant to the universe than a grain of sand to the Earth . . . as a single atom to the Earth.

She couldn't see the stars from her hideaway; if it wasn't the trees hiding them in the summer, it was the clouds keeping the tiny spots up there hidden. The rare occasion when the stars were present depressed her, reminding her that nothing really mattered in the grand scheme. It was an internal battle, this existential crisis of trying to live her life in a way that made her happy while wrestling with the knowledge that, no matter what she did or didn't do, none of it really mattered.

It was those kinds of moments that caused Shirley to get long-winded in her journal entries. She would go on, page after page, about how she couldn't understand the meaning of human life on Earth. It also made her more observant, to question more. When she would get under those trees, soaking up energy from her aged oak, there were ants, mosquitos, caterpillars, gnats, flies and butterflies, and, when she dug, worms, other hidden life down there under the dead leaves and a few thin layers of soil. What was the point in it all? It was thinking like this that made it seem as though she would kill herself, but it didn't last very long. It took such a small creature doing an extraordinary task to shift her dark thinking. Sitting against the trunk of her oak tree, her gaze shifted as if the bark itself had whispered in her ear to look down, where a small black ant carried a chunk of leaf nearly the ant's full size toward the entrance of its colony. The implanted image of Christ hauling the cross flashed in her mind for only a split-second. The ant tried to move in a straight line, but the weight of the leaf made it sway, throwing it off course, but it always got back to the scent path and trudged toward the entrance. When it got there, the struggle worsened. It couldn't get the bit of leaf into the hole, but it didn't give up. It kept forcing that shard forward until another ant (*Barabbas*, she thought) emerged to help, using their mandibles to cut the leaf shard in half, then each took a half into the colony. That the ant hauled such a large leaf to the entrance was remarkable. It succeeded and never gave up. It accepted help. Both were working to help the colony, not allowing themselves one moment's rest until they had completed their task, no matter how small or insignificant. Witnessing this sparked Shirley to begin her own path. It wasn't enough to have a sanctuary a few hundred yards from her house; she had to get out of the county, the state, the entire region. She wrote in her journal that an ant carrying a leaf to its ant hole made her an atheist, made her plan to leave Tennessee forever, and made her accept her own insignificance on Earth and in the universe. It was followed by "haha," but that didn't take away the importance of the experience. She went on to write three pages explaining what she meant, that she wouldn't let her own insignificance prevent her from experiencing joy and satisfaction, almost sensing that she needed to further explain herself, that there would be a reader of her journals that shouldn't be kept in the dark.

iv

Once Autumn had set in, Shirley had, like she had every day, wandered to her oak tree surrounded by the pines. The crackle of fallen leaves underfoot mixed with the hint of chill that had finally broken the heat leftover from summer left Shirley feeling liberated. There was something about the hot and humid air that weighed her down, made each breath seem labored, and left her feeling oppressed. This air, she thought, had traveled all the way down from northern Canada and had finally entered her lungs, cooling her warm body and unlocking the manacles of summer. It had the power to make her smile, and she did when she was here alone. It was more difficult when Richard was with her. He didn't understand the importance of Nature, of this sacred space. She knew that, for him, it was just a place to meet his "girlfriend," a place where the pastor, the school, and the parents couldn't see them, so that they could do whatever they wanted to do without others knowing. And, despite his ignorance, Shirley kept him around. There was something nice about knowing that she was in control of it all. If she didn't want to see him one day, then he didn't push it. When she didn't want sex, he backed off quickly, as if to keep moving forward and trying to pressure her would make the whole sin known to his congregation. She knew that he didn't want any of that attention, but she also knew that if their deeds became known she'd be the one blamed for leading him astray, the Jezebel of Knox County.

Shirley was certainly no Jezebel, but her time in the woods did make her want to know more about what was actually surrounding her. Could she eat the small red berries from the bushes on the path to her oak tree? Were the different kinds of mushrooms sneaking up through the groundcover edible? What kind of bush was that over here and what kind of vine over there? Not only had Rachel Carson's book inspired her, but her own experiences in her sanctuary excited her. This mixture of science, of personal experience, of questioning, and of simple observation had ignited her desire to pursue biology, to try and understand all that she could about all of the things growing around her. It became her passion and obsession that year, the act of questioning and understanding, all of which gave her joy amid her acceptance of insignificance, this marriage of science and philosophy.

She wanted to know, so she put in the work to find out. The public library became an endless source for information, helping her identify the berries that should be added to a fruit salad, those that would help with certain illnesses, and those that would kill her. Helping her identify which leaves would help a wound heal more quickly, which would repel pests, and which would give her discomfort or possibly kill her. And, the fungi, the family she would never feel fully comfortable with identifying on her own. How could she know if what she found was a morel, one of the most delicious of the mushrooms she'd ever taste in her life, or if it was a false morel, which could be the last thing she ever tasted in her life? Sketches and pictures in those books gave details and descriptions to help with identification, but she never reached a level of confidence to go foraging on her own and consume. The leaves and berries were a different story. She certainly felt comfortable because there weren't as many that had such a dire consequence should she consume the wrong thing. The most she would have to deal with regarding what grew in the wild in her area was vomiting and a fevered illness that she'd recover from, but the fungi could kill, and the pain and agony that went along with that kind of death scared her. It even made her wary of mushrooms she saw in grocery stores. While she would still eat the basic button mushrooms or portabella mushrooms that were plentiful on grocery store shelves, she maintained skepticism for all others. The pain. The extreme pain. It frightened her. It frightened her far more than the bone-breaking muscle spasms of tetanus. Maybe because it was the horrible aftermath after something pleasant, like gonorrhea after wonderful lovemaking. Tetanus typically occurred after something painful, like stepping on a nail or cutting your hand on a metal fence. There was nothing pleasant on either end. Shirley imagined that the experience of consuming a poisonous mushroom would be like lovemaking . . . so wonderful at first, and then horrible agony afterwards.

At the nursery, Shirley bought seeds for next year: basil, parsley, thyme, tarragon, sage, and several others. Her plan was to have her own tiny herb garden. To continue learning more about how those herbs would keep her free from maladies or help heal her more quickly than what the pharmacist handed her over the cold counter. A librarian had given her an odd look when she checked out a book with the word Witch in the title, but the book only focused on home remedies, on how people could heal themselves using special combinations of herbs, roots, and other free vegetation typically found beyond the first layer of trees in a forest. What caused her more grief was when Richard noticed. It wasn't just adding a few herbs or mushrooms to a sauce, it was making a delicate mixture of numerous plants and roots for tea blends, steam-healing blends, and combining a few aromatic flowers just to ease the mind. As benign and natural as it was to put some plants together, Richard quickly equated it to witchcraft. And, of course, witchcraft was the devil's work, so it ran deep in his soul that Shirley was either possessed or at least under the influence of evil, under the influence of the Prince of this World—Satan. And he wasn't shy about bringing this to light.

"Leviticus tells us," he went on, "that—"

"Do not dare start preaching to me, Richard Simpson." Shirley stood, her thick oak tree watching it all from behind her. "This is my space. It's not a church."

"Okay. I'm sorry, but I just think that all this stuff you've gotten into is starting to go too far. To-to-to just get weird." Richard stood up as well, a few feet in front of Shirley. "I don't understand—"

"Richard, there's nothing that I'm doing that scientists have not done in order to create medicine, that creators have not done to find new scents for products or create new blends of tea." She took a small step forward. "There's nothing satanic about understanding plants and Nature." Sensing his further confusion and imagining that all that was building up in his mind were more quotes from the Old Testament, she put her hand on his belt. "Besides," she said, sliding her hand down his pants and shifting her eyes toward his groin, "what we're doing is equally sinful in the eyes of the Lord." Her eyes shot up, connecting with his. "Isn't that right?"

He wanted to correct her, but her hand was inside his underwear, petting his growing cock. "You win," he said, then leaned forward and kissed her.

⁓

The sex was more furious than it had ever been, and Richard didn't know what to do with the new energy fueling his ego and knocking a few bolts off the cell door he suddenly felt he'd been locked behind for most of his life. It was the first time he hadn't held back the force he'd worried would hurt her. The first time he took charge, turning her around, yanking her panties down to her knees, lifting her green dress, using saliva for quick lubrication, and then shoving himself inside her. This time, with her back to him and her hands gripping the oak tree, Richard gripped her waist with one hand and a handful of her hair with his other, his thrusts fierce, almost angry, and the response was not "stop" or "not so hard." The response was accepting, was calling for more, and he gave as much as he could until a side stitch slowed him down and forced him to a hurried finish. Covered in sweat, he stood there, his throbbing cock still inside her, one hand on his side where the pain still lingered, and the other letting go and hanging limp at his other side. After a few moments, he slid out of her and took a few steps back, but his legs were too weak to keep him up, and he fell to the dirt and leaves and pine needles. With a smile, he lay back, the sound of crunching leaves like the sound of a small wave rolling onto the beach sand, and stared up at the trees. There had been a weight on his shoulders, on his mind, and in his heart that he didn't notice any longer, and she had been the catalyst to this feeling. Richard couldn't think of the word that described how he felt. It wasn't love because he already felt as though he loved her. It wasn't a high, even though he'd never taken drugs or had a drink . . . he just knew that it was something different.

"Liberating, isn't it?"

That was the word! Liberating. Hearing it, he met her eyes with his and could only nod and smile dumbly. That was the weightlessness, the freedom. Liberation.

Shirley pulled up her panties, turned around and leaned against her tree, most of what Richard had left inside her soaking through the cotton, but she didn't care. She had enjoyed it this time, too. Looking down at her exhausted lover, she could tell that something was different.

There was another layer to this liberation—she liked sex . . . she could initiate it . . . she could dominate it . . . Richard would submit. It was after this round of sex that she found confirmation that she was dominant in this relationship, that what she wanted would not be overshadowed by any level of masculinity Richard could put forth, for she maintained control, made sure that nothing happened that she did not want to happen. And she could do it all while making him, her other, feel as though he had the control. The realization put a smile on her face, and she leaned her head back until it met the bark of her oak tree. There, she closed her eyes and only listened as the wind rattled and pulled the leaves overhead. Listened and imagined what it would be like to be up there on the branch, to fall slowly, sliding back and forth like a pendulum until landing on the soil to soon become soil . . .

Just as the universe was seemingly in line with what she wanted, the trauma came.

V

The year of 1982 put Knoxville, Tennessee, on the map. It hosted the World's Fair that year, adding the Sunsphere to Knoxville's skyline and introducing Cherry Coke to Coca-Cola's repertoire. While the World's Fair was set to wow the world with new inventions, new innovations in science and technology like touchscreen tech, and have a country like Saudi Arabia highlight solar power rather than petroleum, it only brought trauma to Shirley. At the same time that she had found the only place that gave her ease, peace, and solace, the city had, unbeknownst to her, been planning different infrastructure projects that would bring her to tears. Her sanctuary, headed by her large oak tree, more like an altar, and that land under the trees, where she ventured to nearly every day, would be invaded by men. Men driving bulldozers. Men using chainsaws. Men forcing their way through the woods, taking down any tree in the way, and eventually clearing all vegetation in order to put in a new highway, I-640. It was this highway that would not only rip through her sanctuary with no care or worry, but also this highway that would solidify her calling to stop this raping of the land. A place that gave such peace and hope and energy . . . it would now bring pollution, blaring horns, angry people yelling.

She was writing in her journal another endless paragraph about an injustice. This time, her history class teacher and the book they were required to read and take as fact. She had given a presentation on Christopher Columbus, but, rather than follow the specific guidelines to use material from the textbook, Shirley had spent time finding books about Columbus and his voyages across the Atlantic in the library and reading through them in the same place she now wrote in her journal or later in her bedroom. After she had claimed that the textbook was mere propaganda and had started giving several accounts of Columbus not being the discoverer of America, not being this hero that she had been led to believe, and not being a moral human being due to his part in slavery and genocide of indigenous peoples, the teacher cut her off.

"Ms. Wells, you're straying outside the assignment guidelines," Mr. Prest said.

"But—"

"And, you've exceeded your time, so please take a seat."

Shirley didn't understand if this was happening because Mr. Prest was apathetic and ready to get through the presentations or if he was just stopping her before she or others could ask questions that he probably didn't know the answers to. It was probably a little bit of both. But, now, she wanted to ask *him* a question. She wanted to know if *he* knew about these other parts of the Columbus story and, if so, why *he* chose to ignore them. Was he required to follow the class textbook and this book only? When she opened her mouth to try and ask a question, he cut her off again.

"Ms. Taylor."

No one moved or said a word.

"Beth!" he yelled. "Let's hear what you have to say about Magellan."

THE THING IN THE WIND

This yell seemed to break the trance other students were in, and Beth stood up to give her short presentation.

Shirley stared daggers at Beth, watching the girl walk sheepishly toward her. When she reached the front of the classroom, Shirley let her two-page report drop to the floor, casually approached her desk, slid her pen, notebook, and textbook from the top of her desk into her bookbag, then, without even a glance toward Mr. Prest, left the room. She did it all silently, but in her mind, she thought, *So they will try to treat me the same way they treated my mother, but I wonder how far they'll go. And through what means? It won't be the church.* Something told her that Mr. Prest would not follow her or really do anything until after class, at which time he'd probably tell the vice principal that she'd left, which is exactly what had happened.

History had been her first class, so it was quite early when Shirley walked out of school that day, the dew still weighing down the grass and reflecting the sun. The walk home felt so good—the chill a bit more penetrating, an easterly breeze, and morning traffic at a minimum. Under her oak tree, her seat was dry and inviting. And she took it, taking the time to recount what had happened. It was one of the few entries that she would not be able to finish. At just past the halfway point, four men appeared.

"Excuse me, ma'am," said the tallest one.

She had been so engaged with writing that she hadn't heard them approach, and the voice startled her and she dropped her pen and journal.

He was holding a roll of yellow warning tape that she only associated with crime scenes.

"We're going to need you to vacate the premises, please."

Her gut knew what this was, but her mind didn't want to listen, didn't want to believe it. The tingling began in her chest, in the region surrounding her heart. It was like a million tiny electrical wires had all started squirming at the same time, the kind of current that doesn't shock you, but that low vibration that's more like a hum. It surrounded her heart, giving a sensation of closing in and smothering that organ that kept her alive. But, regardless if her gut knew it, she would have to hear it. The man holding that fucking tape would have to say it.

"Why?" she managed to ask, throat as dry as desert sand. Shirley knew that if he was too stupid to know what she was asking she'd not be able to say it without breaking down. Thankfully, he wasn't.

"We're beginning this portion of the I-640 expansion." He smiled after saying this, showing off a nearly toothless grin. "Should have this cleared and out of your way in less than a week."

The words horrified her, but she kept her composure. She collected her journal, got up, took up her bookbag, and made for her house. On the outside, she looked more robotic than human, but, inside, Shirley would later describe this short journey back to her home the same way a person on death row might feel on the way to the electric chair . . . Old Sparky.

In her room, she wept. On the pages in her journal, readers would see the tear stains that had fallen down on the ink and swirled the letters together.

That construction man had been right. The area had been cleared in one week. Richard had been with her the day her oak tree was cut down. She didn't cry that day, just remained stoic while the construction crew cleared out the only place that had ever made her feel at ease, made her feel whole. The way she described it was that it would be a trauma she'd never recover from, and a blight brought on by humans that she would never forgive.

I can't explain it properly, but my oak tree gave me peace. It was like a sponge, soaking up my negative energy and stress, and it never asked for anything in return, as if my company alone was all it desired. It would take on all of that anger and rage, all of that anxiety and sadness, and it would remain there, my silent friend, standing confidently and supportive. I suppose they all did that, all the trees around here, but this was the only one that seemed to call to me that first day I wandered into this place. I've mentioned it before, but it's worth repeating that this was the place that made Tennessee bearable. Once the shackles of adolescence are shed and I'm free, I will leave this place. They've taken away the only space I love, that I care about, like hordes of barbarians invading a village and burning it to the ground. There's nothing more for me here. Mom and Dad seem to have entered that final stage of unbearableness. I wouldn't be surprised if they end up killing each other once I'm gone, so sayeth the Lord. And Richard will be fine. It probably won't take him very long to realize that I just don't dig him very much. Since his liberation, as I've already put down several times, he is a slightly changed

THE THING IN THE WIND

boy, but I know it's only because of me. He needs someone that wants to settle down and start a family, be a housewife or something very close to it. I'm not that. And there's not many like me around here, so that means his liberation has an expiration date. But, I have to thank him for being there for me when the horde came through and destroyed my sanctuary. He even pulled me a little bit closer to him when the oak tree came crashing down. It was an old and sturdy tree, but it was no match for chainsaws and bulldozers. It tried, but it was on the ground in fifteen minutes. I know that it was all in my mind, but, as it fell, I thought I heard it scream out and then weep before it died. Before it was murdered. I know that it wasn't the sound of wood cracking, of it ripping leaves and branches from neighboring trees, or the whine of machinery. I also know that it wasn't the sound from one of the men down there . . . it wasn't a sound that a human could make. This was something older. It was almost like I heard it on a frequency humans weren't programmed to be able to hear, that my antenna was allowed to be adjusted for just a few seconds because the Universe said it'd be okay. I'll never forget it, that scream. That weeping. It had been alive. We had made a connection. The deep sadness that I feel is not so much for it having been cut down, but that I hadn't fought for it, hadn't tried to stop any of it from happening. I knew that it would have been a futile effort, but maybe it was just the point of trying that would have made the difference. Because I hadn't tried to stop it from happening, it would haunt me, one of those "I wish I would have . . ." moments of my past. The tall man with the police tape. He was the one that made me leave. He was the one that supervised clearing out my sanctuary. He had a thick mustache, a dark brown color that matched his eyes. His hair was long, down a few inches from his shoulders, and curling near the bottom. His mouth hadn't seen a toothbrush in years, maybe never. He used words that seemed official, but the confidence level in his tone and the stupid look on his face made it clear that he didn't have a full understanding of the words he spoke: "Vacate the premises" . . . did he even know what premises meant? So many of them were so stupid, but they had the power over the land, over Nature, and, like Mr. Prest, over how education would work . . . that spreading lies was okay. The human race was stupid. Well, mostly stupid. If Rachel Carson was alive, I'd really

23

like to meet her and just have a conversation. The others, parents included, I don't need to interact with them anymore. That would be fine with me. And poor Richard. He doesn't know he's just following a pattern. I guess none of them do. I don't want to follow that pattern, and I won't. Today was full of atrocity, humans not at their worst, but on that side of the coin. What kind of person would I be if I tried to equate the Holocaust, use of nuclear bombs in Japan, or those sorts of terrible human acts with knocking down some trees to put in a highway? I can see this entry devolving into blabbing, so I will stop here. Until next time, my dear.

It didn't take the city long to flatten the area and turn it into I-640, a busy bypass that eliminated the quietness and peacefulness of her neighborhood, but it did help it grow more quickly, so businesses, churches, and the schools liked the addition. Shirley felt as if she was the only one that despised it, the only one that saw it as a vector for more pollution, more noise, and more devouring of resources. But, most of all, she felt like she was the only one that had lost something. It had been her chapel, her sanctuary, her backyard. None of the others in the neighborhood had lost anything, so they couldn't empathize. Maybe if the city had wanted to tear down some homes, businesses, and churches, then it would have mattered.

So, she lamented. Already an introvert albeit her recent rebellion, she simply calculated the number of days before she could leave and gained tunnel vision toward that day, high school graduation. There weren't many options for her. If she just picked up and left, she would arrive in a new place with little money, no job, and nowhere to stay. While part of her knew that it'd be better than staying, she also knew that it shouldn't be considered an option. The only real option was college. And she would need a scholarship, so she focused on that and only that. It was her ticket out of there.

On Friday, two weeks after her sanctuary had been destroyed, Shirley couldn't go home, couldn't stand the thought of it, so she visited Greenwood Cemetery, a place she would describe in her journal as *bland, but it was quiet. I wish there were more trees. I don't care that the tombstones are mostly basic, but the lack of trees. I miss my trees.* She walked along the boneyard paths like one might a track, trying to keep it together. It only worked for about ten minutes. That's when Shirley stopped and sat down by the nearest headstone, Cathcart: Born 1897. Died 1970. And she wept. Just whimpering and light tears. That deep inner pain inside her, that sense of not belonging, that she was the outsider and left unwanted . . . it all surfaced and pulled her down. Who was she? Why didn't she matter? And then came the second wave. When that realization hit her, it did so with the weight of granite. It was the first time in her life, at least the time of her life that she could remember, that she bellowed out a howl, followed by a flood of tears that only those in the darkest of places could shed. She screamed and cried and screamed some more. It felt like her abdomen was ripping away from her ribcage, that tears were forming in her stomach lining, that her throat was on fire, and that her lips, stretching to their capacity, would rip open at any moment. Her thoughts were incoherent, a jumble of melancholic images of her life, of her situation. All of it hit her at once, like the rising pressure from deep within the earth, pushing and pushing until it forms a volcano and erupts. This was her eruption. It was no spilling over like Mount Etna; this was Mount St. Helens or Mount Vesuvius. And when the ash settled, when she regained control of herself, she had reached a new level. She had rebelled against her teachers, her parents, her town, her church. She had found a sanctuary and started thinking for herself, started making her existence in this place bearable, started learning about ways to heal and be one with Nature. She had learned how to use rebellion, learned how to go after what she wanted, even if it went against societal norms, and learned to block out cultural influences. It was her rebirth.

When the tears no longer flowed and when she was in control of her emotions again, Shirley began laughing, laughing like a madwoman. It only lasted for maybe ten seconds, but it was hysterical. Of all that could have been on her mind, it was a few lines she remembered from the King James version of the Holy Bible: "Lazarus, come forth. And he that was dead came forth, bound hand and foot with graveclothes: and his face was bound about with a napkin. Jesus saith unto them, Loose him, and let him go."

"I am in a cemetery, after all," Shirley said, stifling her laughter. "Whether they'll understand it or not, I shall be Lazarus, but they won't know that I was dead until they're all dead to me."

She read the quote on the Cathcart tombstone: "Fear not them which kill the body, but are not able to kill the soul: but rather fear him which is able to destroy both soul and body in hell."

The quote, she remembered coming from somewhere in Matthew, made her think that this man had been murdered. It was the only explanation. And here she was, weeping atop a murdered man. Regardless of her struggles, she was better off than that poor bastard. Letting out a deep breath, she got to her feet.

"Thank you for indulging me, Mr. Cathcart. I'll be on my way now."

When Shirley left Greenwood Cemetery, it would be the last time she'd weep like that. It would be the last time she would ever let herself be in a place that she didn't want to be in. The hour she had spent in the cemetery, she knew, had been the final element needed for her to shed her skin and to move forward. She shed Richard, who took the split pretty well, realizing that they didn't have a place for sex anymore. At least she thought he'd taken it well, but she'd never really know. Her parents didn't notice her change, so that made her putting even more distance between her and them much easier. Her father maintained his level of drinking and violence. Her mother, whom she wished would just take her aside and talk to her and open up at least once, remained closed off to her and defensive when her father got violent. At school, she stopped speaking in classes, stopped any attempts to connect with other students, and stopped questioning teachers. Her only focus was finishing high school and getting the hell out of Tennessee, getting far away from Bible Belt culture, and getting her new life started somewhere else.

As she withdrew, Shirley gained even more insight and understanding of those around her. She had gone from expressing what she saw as issues to being an observer. It was amazing what one could learn (or infer) by just watching. In first period, half the class was bored and tired. A quarter of them were attentive most of the time. The remaining quarter were the interesting bunch. A few, Molly Miller and Henry Bowman, had clearly done all the work, knew a bit more than what the textbook had to say, and were the perfect little students, taking notes and paying attention. A few others were goofing off, like Zach Aldridge, who kept passing slips of paper with stupid jokes to those sitting around him. But, then there was Beth Taylor. This one had clearly not done the read and did not take notes. Instead, she sat there, hair in pigtails, gazing at

THE THING IN THE WIND

Mr. Prest, eraser-end of her pencil in her mouth. Shirley enjoyed watching this, the way Beth made Mr. Prest divert his eyes or get flushed cheeks when she licked the pencil tip with her tongue. It may have just been flirtation, but Shirley felt that it was more, and she knew that she could stir up a heavy dose of revenge and drama if she wanted to. But, she didn't want to. She just enjoyed observing, learning how people reacted to surprises, to jokes, to human anatomy and its reproductive elements, to war, to desire, to boredom. She watched this for months, finally being able to understand the definition of the human condition. If that was the case, then where did she fit in? She was a human studying humans. It was a question that she didn't know how to answer, so she left it hanging here.

VI

Shirley was not selected for three of the scholarships she had applied for, but she was asked to give an interview for the fourth. The opening questions were standard, but then the man asked her something that had not been in the prep guides for these kinds of interviews. He asked her why she wanted to stray so far from home. She paused for nearly fifteen seconds as her mind erupted. After having done much observation of her teachers, classmates, parents, and those around the neighborhood, she realized that the South had a way of keeping people close, like the South was a huge magnet and the people were made of iron. They couldn't get away even if they wanted to because the grip of family and religion had its talons sunken in deep. But, Shirley was something different, a body of titanium, immune to the pull of family and religion, too strong for talons to penetrate. She was a stranger there, an outsider, and getting far away was the only option, scholarship or not.

She thought it best not to say all of this to the interviewer, but she did tell him about shifting her focus a bit, becoming the observer and learning how to take in all that data and learn from it.

The interviewer, Bruce Rheims, a fifty-two-year-old professor with no hair on the top of his head but plenty on his face, sat back in his chair and crossed his arms. "An observer, huh?" He chuckled. "Well, Ms. Shirley Wells, I think that's the best answer I've gotten to that question in a long time. Science is all about observation, pulling in data, testing, and blah, blah, blah." He smiled, a healthy and full set of teeth showing for the first time in the interview. "Thank you for your time." He stood.

Shirley felt anxiety creep in, not sure what it all meant. Why did he cross his arms? It contradicted his smile and the words coming out of his mouth.

Standing and uncrossing his arms, Bruce extended his hand.

Shirley stood as well, taking his strong and dry hand in her cold and clammy one.

"You'll be hearing from us within the next few weeks," he said, then winked as he let go of her hand. "You go and enjoy the rest of your day."

And she did. She went home, went to her room, and filled pages in her journal. It took only eight days to get a response from the scholarship committee. They had offered her a full ride to the University of Washington in Seattle, the farthest she could get from Tennessee and still be in the continental United States. Hallelujah and praise the Lord!

She accepted, but she kept it all from her parents. How would she deal with that? While it seemed harsh, the best scenario she could think of was just disappearing. Leave a note so they knew she was not kidnapped, but keep it vague, then take a taxi to the bus station. She could fit her necessities into one large suitcase and overnight bag. The scholarship would take care of everything else—room, board, and tuition. She would probably need to get a job for extra money, but that was for Seattle. No need to worry about those kinds of things now. And that was precisely what she did.

vii

August 1983. Shirley exited the back door of her home and walked until she reached the shoulder of I-640. Engines roared past her, bellowing out their foul and fetid fumes, nearly choking her. Car after car and truck after truck, they all went by without a care in the world, without an understanding of what this used to be, of what had happened here. It was the eastbound side, right lane and shoulder . . . that's where her peaceful sanctuary's altar, her oak tree, used to be, right in the middle of all this chaos. Is that what people were going to end up doing? Stripping away every natural sanctuary for another highway? Have no respect for anything that stood in the way? It filled her with rage. It reminded her of Rachel

THE THING IN THE WIND

Carson's *Silent Spring* again. That woman had observed humanity taking steps in the wrong direction with herbicide and pesticide use, so was she seeing a different kind of terrible step, toward urban sprawl? There would be no book written, but she would damn sure put it in her journal. But it was not easy because she saw the contradiction here. In a few hours, she would be boarding a bus that would take her over 2,000 miles across the country using highways, taking her away from all that she abhorred in Knoxville.

When she couldn't take it any longer, Shirley turned her back on the highway, the flat tombstone of her refuge, and went back home. On the way, she thought again of Young Goodman Brown. His life before the journey was full of hope and happiness, even if he was living behind a veil. His journey, his enlightenment, it all led him to truth, at least from his perspective, and it broke him. To see the world beyond the veil meant seeing that it was mostly deplorable, the same way Shirley had noticed her classmates and teachers once she stepped back and shifted to observing. What she saw wasn't pleasant, but it was the truth. And she was okay with that. She wanted the truth over anything else. Furthermore, it was her truth that had gotten her the scholarship that would transport her away from all this. Would it be the same elsewhere? Would all parts of the United States be the same, with regard to the human condition, or would there be differences, nuances, anything that would give her hope of a better place? Shirley was hopeful. And when she called the taxi, she hoped that her parents would not get home early and spoil her plan. They didn't, and she left the letter for them on the dining room table.

The Greyhound bus was nearly full, was not comfortable, but it was reliable. It left Knoxville and began its journey across the country to the edge of the continent.

CHAPTER 2:
BERIN VAN TIGHEM

i

GROWING UP IN a community that welcomed over a million vacationers each year made business owners smile and many residents cringe, but not the van Tighem family. Berin and his brother Frank lived together in a two-story house overlooking the Bow River in Banff, Alberta. The brothers' parents had died in a boating accident on Lake Minnewanka the winter after Berin had finished high school, so Berin took on the role of father for the two years it took Frank to finish up school. And then there was the girl, Julia Calvert, the one that lived on the other side of the river near the hot springs and Rimrock Resort. She and Berin had started dating their junior year of high school. It took Julia a month to fall in love with Berin, twenty-nine days longer than it had taken Berin to fall in love with her. The first real test of their relationship came right after high school when Julia relocated to Calgary to pursue a degree in engineering at the University of Calgary. It was only an hour-and-a-half drive, but it might as well have been across the country. While she was reading, taking exams, reading more, and trying to stay on point through various labs, Berin shuttled tourists from various hotels and resorts to other resorts, ski slopes, Lake Louise, and, if he was lucky, the bus to and from Calgary International Airport. It was on those trips to the airport that he usually found a way to have lunch or dinner with his Julia if she was available. In the off-season, Berin worked as a bartender at the Maple Leaf Bar down by the bridge that used to take him to his Julia.

Once Frank had graduated, Berin didn't hesitate to make the

move to Calgary. His experience as a chauffeur quickly landed him a position with Alberta Limousine and Shuttle, which found him spending most of his time somewhere in the city rather than the countryside. It paid enough for him to afford a small apartment near the university where he and Julia could live together for the first time, even though they kept this part from her parents. While Julia said that her parents would not raise an eyebrow too high, they would probably raise it some, and she didn't want them to have any reason to dislike or look down on Berin.

Julia was a top-notch student and graduated a year early because of all the summer courses she had completed. At a small graduation party, which was held on St. Patrick's Island—a 31-acre block of land in the middle of the Bow River that passed through the heart of Calgary—in front of Julia's parents and friends, in front of Frank, Berin knelt to one knee.

"Julia, I'm so proud of you, my love. We're here, on this island that splits the river that used to separate us. It followed us from Banff to Calgary. Behind me, our split river becomes one. It joins together without conflict or worry. It becomes a mighty force that never succumbs to obstacles in its path." He reached into his pocket and pulled out the black velvet box containing the engagement ring. As he opened it, he looked up into her hazel eyes. They were brimming with salty tears, just waiting for the right moment to stream down her face and onto the ground where this man that she loved waited. "Join me, my sweet Julia. Make me the happiest man on this vast planet." He knew that he'd have to hurry with the question . . . her fighting to keep the tears contained began to fail. "Will you marry me, Julia? Will you—"

She fell to her knees, the first deluge smearing her makeup, dark streaks immediately soaring down her face. "Yes!" she said. "Yes!" Her hands were upon his, covering them and the ring. "I . . . will . . . marry . . . you." She could barely get the words out between sniffles and sobs.

Berin only smiled and let a few tears sneak from his eyes as well.

"I will marry you," she said again, then touched his forehead with her own. "I love you."

Berin closed his eyes, feeling her hot heavy breath on his face, feeling the fiery heat from her forehead bring his to sweat, feeling the cool tears graze his cheek and fall onto his cupped hands.

They stayed that way for a while before he laughed, no, he giggled, then said, "Can I put the ring on your finger, my love?"

She laughed at this, then leaned back, a face full of smeared makeup, sweat, tears, and snot. When they made eye contact again, she said, "Are you sure you want to marry me? I'm a mess."

He didn't respond verbally. He took the ring and slid it onto her left ring finger.

Not wanting to make a spectacle or spend a lot of money, they were married a month later on the shore of the Bow River back home in Banff along the Bow River Trail. Frank attended, along with Julia's parents. They'd agreed to postpone the honeymoon until she was finished with college.

Julia had applied for the master's program at University of Alberta in Edmonton, was accepted, and had her tuition paid for when she was accepted as a graduate assistant. It was another move, but one that happened smoothly due to Berin's connections in the service industry. His boss connected him with a former associate, Gerry Hamilton, who had the largest limousine and shuttle service in Edmonton. It would be two years before their lives would change again.

ii

Alberta is one of the more diverse provinces in Canada. In the southwest are the Canadian Rockies, full of skiers, hikers, tourists, recreation, and all the things vast mountains provide. The middle of the province, the bottom half, has the major cities of Edmonton and Calgary for those desiring the city life and all that city life has to offer. It's the upper half that makes it much more different than the others. Not necessarily the north and northwest with its lakes, wildlife, forests, bogs, and desolation—that is quite the norm. But in the east, centered at Fort McMurray and running along the Athabasca River, an industrial project so vast an astronaut can see it from space, one finds the largest industrial project on the planet . . . one finds the Alberta Tar Sands. Thirst for oil caused big oil companies to begin large-scale production, wiping away vast swaths of muskeg land to excavate the bitumen through open pit mining, extract the crude oil from the mix of sand, clay, and water, then refine it.

The tar sands production operations quickly turned what was

once a bogland full of trees and plants and wildlife into a vast wasteland devoid of vegetation, the only towering trees replaced by smokestacks, the wetlands replaced with tailings ponds full of oil sands waste. Of course, it didn't prevent all of the pollution from getting into the Athabasca River. It quickly registered on environmentalists' radars after the first complaints and health concerns surfaced from First Nations communities downriver . . .

Julia had nearly finished the second draft of her thesis when her advisor called her in for a meeting.

"I have what might be very good news for you, Julia," said Professor Annette Helson, pausing to smile her goofy smile and brush a few curls that had loosened from her ponytail. "We have a lot of contact with Shell and Suncor, and they want to offer you and two others a job once you've finished up your degree this May." She leaned forward for emphasis when she added, "A job, Julia, not an internship."

Julia was speechless. She hadn't even started considering where she wanted to work, if she wanted to stay in Alberta, in Canada, or even on the continent.

"You're at the top of your class, and we all know it. You'll have an official interview if you're interested in moving in this direction, but know that, just between us, they're expecting to start your position in six figures."

She was still speechless, her mouth opening involuntarily.

"You don't have to answer now, but they want to know if you're interested by the end of next week. The job is in Fort McMurray. Even includes a housing stipend." Already anticipating a question, Professor Helson added, "And there are opportunities for your husband as well, which is as far as they went with that, but certainly something that'll get more explanation should you interview."

Knowing that she had to say something, Julia just let out, "Thank you so much. I need to give this some thought and would like to talk to Berin about it, too."

"Of course. Yes! Please do so." She finally sat back in her chair, smile fading. "I look forward to your thoughts once you're ready."

~⌒⌒◠

When Berin got home, she was on the loveseat, three bottles of beer ahead of him.

"Bad day?" he asked, fully prepared to be supportive. It was a role he had grown used to when she had to vent or wanted to talk through an issue in class or on her thesis.

Unlike Professor Helson, she felt completely comfortable expressing herself to Berin. "Yeah, I think so." She finished the half bottle of beer and asked him to get her another. "You should probably get one for yourself, too."

He chugged one, then got a second for himself. Julia didn't usually have bad news, so he didn't know just how bad it would be. He figured that if it was a death, that she'd be sad. If it was a bad grade or negative feedback on a chapter of her thesis, then it'd be pure anger. But this was some odd mixture of worry, anger, sadness, and, what was that other one? Resentment? Whatever it was, she hadn't expressed it in his presence in the years that they'd known each other.

"I'm ready . . . let it out," he said after handing her a beer and sitting next to her on the loveseat.

She took a sip, turned to him, and said with menace, "So, I was told that I was the top student in the program and got offered a job that pays six figures today."

When she paused, Berin didn't respond, didn't change expression, just sat there, waiting, somehow knowing that it couldn't be all of the story. If that was the whole story, then it was great news.

"It's right here in Alberta. You'd be able to find work that I assume would pay well."

Was that it? Was she wanting to get out of Alberta and this big opportunity would keep her here?

She took in a mouthful of Molson and swallowed it, clenching her teeth as it went down. "It's Fort McMurray, the tar sands. They want me to work for Big Oil. I don't know what I'd be doing specifically, but they want me to work for big fucking oil." She shook her head. "Big Oil in Fort McMurray where they're completely destroying and devastating every inch of the environment."

And there it was, finally. They had spoken significantly about her desire to focus her expertise on sustainable energy solutions, not be part of the destructive ones. Berin knew that there was only one proper response to this, and he gave it: "I support any decision you make. I'm completely behind you, no matter what."

THE THING IN THE WIND

"I know you are, Berin!"

Oops . . . he shouldn't have said anything.

"I'm just trying to get my thesis finished so I can finish up the program, but now I have to drive myself crazy looking for what's available elsewhere. I don't want to go to Fort McMurray! I don't want to work for Oil! God dammit!"

This time, he didn't respond.

"Would I be a hypocrite if I took the job and only stayed a few years just for the money? Use the time to find the perfect place with a company that matters, that's doing good things?"

Now he was in a no-win situation, so he gave a quick answer: "I trust that you know what's best here, Julia. I mean, just because you work for a company doesn't mean that you subscribe to their message or standards. I don't know what your role would be, but you might be just what they need."

"What do you mean by that?"

"If you're in an influential position, you might be able to prevent some of the damage they could cause in the future."

She tilted her head, then said, "That hadn't occurred to me. Of course! I don't have to work for some sustainable energy producer to be part of the cause." A sly smile emerged. "I could be part of the enemy, almost like a spy or saboteur . . . stop some of the damage. I'm not automatically a traitor if I work for them."

Berin didn't choose to add anymore to the conversation at that point. He only hoped that his input would lead to the best possible outcome, that he wouldn't regret putting in his two cents to this conversation. Of course, he wouldn't know until she made the decision and they moved forward. However, the immediate response was one that he was very happy with. He saw the tension leave her shoulders as she exhaled a deep, beer-soaked breath, then leaned to him and nestled her face in the crook of his neck. The stress must have exhausted her because she was asleep in a few minutes. And Berin barely moved, finishing his beer and the beer he'd rescued from her hand before her grip could loosen and let it drop on the loveseat. Not long after, he, too, was asleep.

When he woke, Julia was gazing at him, the fingers on her right hand sliding through his hair. He had no idea what time it was, but noticed that it was dark outside.

"If you keep doing that," he said, "you'll put me right back to sleep." And he smiled.

"I love you, Berin." She did not stop running her fingers through his dark hair, knowing that it was one of his favorite things. "You really are my other half." She kissed him softly. "Thank you for all of your patience." She kissed him again. "And for coming with me on this journey, giving up your life in Banff." She kissed him again. "And—"

He kissed her this time, then carried her to the bedroom. They made love slowly. And when they were done, eyes locked, he said, "I'd go anywhere with you. You are my love, always."

There were no more words spoken that night, only holding each other as they drifted into a deep and peaceful sleep.

The following day, Julia entered Professor Helson's office and told her that she'd be honored to move forward with the interview, and so plans were set in motion. She ended up with Suncor, and she and Berin relocated to Fort McMurray a few weeks after her graduation, leaving Edmonton and never venturing back.

...

iii

The urban service area of Fort McMurray sits where the Clearwater River runs into the Athabasca River, a place known chiefly for petroleum. When Julia and Berin arrived, they rented an apartment in the Timberlea neighborhood, just across the river from the center of Fort McMurray. While Berin was qualified for and offered a few jobs by Suncor, he chose to go a different route. He got involved in the tourism industry, focusing mostly on river excursions and private transport. Neither of them liked Fort McMurray, even though the petroleum companies certainly did more to keep workers safe, limit the impact their operations had on the environment, and help the surrounding communities than those both Julia and Berin had read about in African countries, where there was far more exploitation and corruption.

The marriage was strong. Even if either had had a rough day, they always greeted each other with a smile and hug and kiss, followed by dinner and conversation. After just two years, Julia had been promoted twice, elevating her job status a bit, but mostly elevating her pay. She was climbing quickly, and she noted that meetings were soon attended by higher-ups, and then more higher-ups, to the point that they were all using first names only by the end of year three.

THE THING IN THE WIND

"I knew that we were making the right decision to offer you a position," said the executive vice president after a meeting.

The comment confused Julia slightly. How could that have been the case if they hadn't met her? Did her professors have that much influence?

"Why? If you don't mind my asking?"

"Your thesis," he said. "It was top-notch, even the first draft version that we were given when we made the decision." After what sounded like a fake laugh, he added, "And it was anonymous."

"Thank you," she said. And it was sincere, a "thank you" that was not only directed at him and whoever else made the decision to consider her for the position, but a "thank you" to her professor for keeping it all based on expertise, knowledge, aptitude . . . not gender and physical appearance. It was a longstanding fear of hers, but her colleagues and bosses were surprisingly not interested in those kinds of games, at least not with her. It wasn't something she ever brought up with Berin, but she mentioned it once to the only other female with executive status, Melinda Baker, after she had gotten to know her for nearly a year.

"Well, that's because their focus is production and money, honey. Don't think it's not on their minds," Melinda had responded.

That night at dinner, she brought up a topic that made Berin squirm. "We've been here three years, Berin, and I'm moving up quickly."

"I know, sweetheart, and I'm so proud of you." He meant it. It was all sincere. However, each step up the ladder she'd taken had been a giant leap away from her original plan, her original desires for a clean and healthy planet, sustainable energy. But he didn't dare open that Pandora's box.

"Do you think we should consider buying a place up here?"

There it was. She might as well have asked him if he'd like for her to take hot coals from a campfire and see how they'd feel on his eyes, in his throat, down his pants.

"I'd love to hear your thoughts."

"Well, I don't know." She giggled, then smiled when she continued, "I thought a house would be nice if we wanted to start a family."

That was new. She hadn't talked about children. Hell, Berin didn't even know if she really wanted children. So much of her focus over the past decade had been school and work. But here it was.

"Are you trying to tell me something?" he asked. Of all the places on Earth, this was near the bottom of the list of places he'd ever want to have a pregnant wife or to try and raise a child— surrounded by one of the most dangerous industries!

"Maybe not what you think, but maybe you want to start trying?"

Berin could see how the thought filled her with happiness, the first time he'd seen this level of happiness in her since their time in Calgary. There was no way he'd stand in the way of her happiness, so he agreed, and they bought a house and moved in three months later. It wasn't long after that Julia got pregnant. And she kept working, making a name for herself within Suncor and snagging the attention of some of Suncor's competitors. But, as the child, who would be named Berin if a boy or Daniela if a girl, continued to grow, Julia got weaker. And when the child was stillborn, it crushed her. All the promotions Suncor could offer would not pull her from the level of grief she felt when her first child had died inside her. As much as she didn't want to say it or think it, she knew that her job was to blame. Fort McMurray did so many wonderful things for so many people financially, but those that had to stay there, those who lived there or around there, they were the sacrifices to expanding bank accounts.

Berin did not express anything but concern and care for his wife. He knew the risks, but he also wanted to keep a smile on Julia's face, to give her everything she could ever want. But not this! This was a lifelong prescription for grief, remorse, and other emotions that had a way of keeping people down. Berin didn't know what to do except just be there. He couldn't pressure her into leaving the job. What would they do? Where would they go? Maybe it didn't matter, but he didn't bring it up nevertheless. He just accepted that, as long as they stayed in Fort McMurray, as long as she worked for a company that practiced what Berin and Julia did not believe in, they would be stuck. There would always be some element seeming a bit off or broken. Until they were both on the path that they both desired, deep down, there'd be conflict and unnecessary challenges thrown their way. But this! This was not just a challenge. This was evil. This could change everything. Deep down, they both knew that the tar sands were to blame.

THE THING IN THE WIND

The corporate office bent over backwards to support her, giving her paid time off, sending flowers and cards, and being supportive in every way a company could be. It was during this time that Berin realized that, while a company was technically its people, it was something else as well. Individually, the employees, the managers, the corporate folk, they were mostly good people; it was when the company as a whole, thinking like a company, as a corporate entity, took control, that was when the darkness slipped in, when the sympathy and empathy disappeared, and when concern for people, the environment, the planet, everything . . . that all disappeared, for the only true CEO of any corporation is Mammon. Thankfully, Julia had been dealing with individuals this time.

After nearly six months off, Julia chose to go back to work. She couldn't stay inside any longer, couldn't get through the day without a drink, two drinks, four drinks . . . she needed to get her focus back. And they welcomed her back with open arms. This was in April 2016. The following month, southwest of Fort McMurray, a fire started. While over one thousand fires occurred in Alberta each year, this one was significant. This one lasted over a year, caused the evacuation of 88,000 people, stymied oil production, and destroyed over 3,000 buildings; however, it (arguably) did not cause any deaths.

That was how the outsiders viewed it. First Nations people saw and felt something far different, something that no white man, no outsider could really understand. They realized that this fire was an awakening, a warning, a sign that told them it was the last straw, the one that broke the camel's back. Those who felt it the most relocated. The others, the ones whose beliefs had wavered from tradition, threw caution to the wind, even though a large forest fire was often a sign.

The following August, when the fire had finally been extinguished, the disappearances, deaths, and other maladies began occurring in the region. For Julia, the end of the fire was the end of her position at Suncor, and she and Berin prepared to relocate. Never knowing how they found out so quickly that she had stepped away from Suncor, Julia was contacted by Forum Energy Metals the following day and offered a position.

"Why am I such a magnet for companies doing things that I'm against?" Julia asked Berin after the phone call. "It's like the universe is trying to keep me from changing the world in a positive way."

"Or it's just another obstacle because doing the right thing is never easy."

They discussed the position over dinner, and she chose to take it because it would get her away from Fort McMurray and because the clean and sustainable energy companies had not responded to her inquiries. It also helped that her pay would be significantly higher than her final position at Suncor.

"These companies certainly don't mind throwing around a lot of money to get what they want."

"They'll still be getting more than what they paid for," said Berin.

The response ignited a fire within her that she hadn't felt since before the pregnancy. They made love that night. It was the last time Berin would feel that close to her. Two days later, Forum had paid for movers to get their belongings to Fort Chipewyan, a small community about 200 kilometers north of Fort McMurray, on the western bank of Lake Athabasca, in a two-bedroom house that they included as part of her signing on. The third day, she was on assignment to Fir Island, Saskatchewan, a chunk of land in Black Lake that Forum wanted to obtain for uranium mining. Julia was to head the group of scientists, begin testing on the island, and then return a week later.

iV

In Banff, Berin had been an outgoing student, a hockey player on the high school team, the Banff Bears. Others liked him, and he liked the others, never saying no to a get-together or to help out a friend. After graduation, he started to change slowly. The extrovert began taking baby steps toward being an introvert. When he'd made the move to Calgary, he lost touch with his friends, with the exception of the occasional phone call. The only person he maintained much contact with was his brother, Frank, who had made connections with the tourism industry and worked as a freelance guide, taking city folk out to fishing locations and hunting locations. Berin had a few acquaintances at Alberta Limousine and Shuttle, but, aside from the occasional beer after work, it had just been him and Julia, when Julia had a moment to spare. When she didn't, he'd do things alone, mostly read, watch a hockey match, or have a few beers. It didn't take long for it to feel normal and okay. The Edmonton move eliminated the work acquaintance element. If it wasn't with Julia (or Julia and classmates), it was just Berin. And he was still okay with that. There was something that kept him feeling at ease when alone, as long as he knew Julia was okay. But the move to Fort McMurray disrupted that ease. Not only was it a place that disturbed and bothered him—a place, of all things, did this, not the people—but the changes he noticed in Julia got under his skin. When she hinted at going against the beliefs she had held so strongly while a student, Berin didn't have to like it, but he felt that he had to be supportive of her wants and desires. And when she got pregnant, he was both elated and terrified. While he certainly loved her and wanted to support her desire for a family, he worried about raising their child in a place like this, about Julia's health, and, in the back of his mind, worried about how he would not have any time to himself anymore—a selfish thought, but it had crept into his mind more than once. And then the child had died.

Berin's only focus had been Julia. He did not leave her side for the entire six months she had grieved, and it was exactly what she needed. Without him, she'd said, she would not have recovered as quickly, maybe not at all. He felt that his part was easy. He didn't say much that half of the year, only listened, gave heartfelt responses when a response was expected, took care of all bills and grocery shopping and cooking, and he held her. That was the most important act . . . he held her. When she cried, he held her. When they went to bed, he held her. When they woke in the morning, he held her. And when she stood on the porch staring out at the trees or just gazed out the window, he was behind her, holding her and letting her know that he was there, that she was not alone in her grief.

On that third day in Fort Chipewyan, in the living room of their new house, she thanked him.

"I wouldn't have been able to move forward without your love." Tears had started falling before she got the first word out. "You are the most wonderful person, Berin. I feel so lucky that you chose to stay with me with all of the moves, living in that hell of Fort McMurray. You've sacrificed a lot for me."

Berin took all of this in as she said it, not responding.

"And I want you to know that I'm grateful. I appreciate you." She closed her eyes, her face wet with tears and streaks of eyeliner.

"This is . . . I want to promise you that this is the last time you'll have to follow me somewhere." She touched his face, her controlled tears approaching uncontrollable. "I won't stay with this company long. And when that time comes, we follow your dreams, okay?"

He had not expected this, but his response was sincere. "My love, I am content if you are happy, so, if you are happy, then I am happy."

"But what about your dreams, Berin? What about what you want?"

"I'm happy with you, Julia. The jobs I've had help with our finances, and they've been just fine as long as I have you."

She smiled at this and then hugged him. "We have over a million dollars in the bank. A short stint with this company should get us pretty well set so that we don't have to worry about money for a very long time."

Later, after she had gathered her bags for the short trip to Fir Island, she embraced him and said, "I'll see you soon. When I get back next week, I think that we should start making some solid plans. Plans that will put us first."

"That sounds nice," he said. He'd felt close to her that day, close the way they were back in Banff. She had shown him that he was important to her, more important than her classes, her research, and her job. That he was the most important element to her life. And it made him feel good, made him feel that the mutual feeling was understood on both sides now.

It made her going away for a week more bearable. After she got into the taxi, Berin didn't want to be alone. Something about the conversation had stirred a change in him, a change that made the thought of being alone unbearable for the first time in years. So, he phoned Frank.

"Frank, if there's a way for you to be up here with me, I'd certainly appreciate it."

Frank had been surprised by this. While his brother had called at least once a week, he'd never pled with Frank to join him, to keep him company. So, Frank packed his bags and headed to Fort Chipewyan the same day, letting the companies he freelanced for know that he'd be unavailable for an unknown amount of time.

When Frank's plane landed in Fort Chipewyan, Berin picked him up and proceeded to talk about the fishing and hunting opportunities in the area, to talk about getting involved in the tourism industry here, and to talk about buying a boat to do it all.

THE THING IN THE WIND

"We have an extra room where you can stay, Frank. You'll see . . . it'll be great!"

Frank obliged, never wanting to let his older brother down. And he didn't mention how odd Berin was acting. He'd not seen his brother just jump to do something on a whim, especially something that would cost a lot of money. Berin had always had some kind of plan, but the way he sounded about this was more like what Frank would expect from a teenager. He needed to see how far Berin would take it before finally asking what had caused this shift in behavior. And to try and stop Berin if it seemed he'd go too far.

"People pay a lot of money to get away. To come up to places like this for fishing and hunting. Hell, just to get out of the city for a long weekend," said Berin.

"And Banff gets more crowded every year."

"Exactly."

Frank didn't want to throw out the painfully obvious issue, but, being a good brother, he had to address it: "I'm a bit surprised that you're considering doing it here."

Berin nodded, got them a few beers from the refrigerator, and said, "Downriver. I know. But, if we focus on the eastern side, all that crap flowing in from the tar sands shouldn't be a factor. And, as for hunting, it should be fine."

"What about—"

"I already know what you're going to say, brother. Don't worry about the money. I'll handle that part of it."

Frank downed half his bottle of Molson and then said, "Fuck it. Let's give it a go."

Over the next few days, they found a used trawler, bought it, and got connected with Athabasca Fishing Tours, a small company with half its boats in need of serious repair. So, the prospect of a few freelancers helping out was all good news according to them. But, by the end of the week, Frank knew that he would be taking on much more responsibility far sooner than expected because Berin received word that his wife was missing.

Berin had not known that seeing his wife get into a taxi a few days ago would be the last time he would see her. The last time he'd hear her voice. The last time he'd feel her in his arms. The last time he'd truly care about anything . . .

Missing! They said that she was missing. How could

43

something like that happen? She had flown to Stony Rapids. There was only one road to Black Lake, where she was to take a boat to Fir Island.

"According to our scientists waiting for her in Black Lake, she didn't make it *to* Black Lake," said the Forum representative. "Neither did our driver. We've already contacted the authorities and a search has commenced."

Julia had just disappeared, along with Forum's local driver. There was no sign of a struggle anywhere along Highway 964, and the few roads that intersected were all checked as well—nothing. It was as if the road had been alive and hungry that day, swallowing them whole and leaving no trace. None of it made sense.

"We've arranged transportation and lodging for you if you'd like to come to Stony Rapids."

"Make it for two," Berin responded.

The search lasted for one week. They had boats in both Lake Athabasca and Black Lake searching, one Eurocopter AS350 Écureuil (Squirrel), four SUVs, and ten Royal Canadian Mounted Police officers. When Berin and Frank landed in Stony Rapids, which covered over one hundred square kilometers of trees, waterways, and an occasional quarry, they were invited to join the helicopter crew, but there was no sign of Julia. When they returned, Berin was met by Sergeant Tate of the RCMP in the lobby of the White Water Inn and Lodge. The man towered over Berin by at least a foot, his blonde hair shiny, his shoulders broad.

"Mr. van Tighem," he said in a booming voice, hand extended.

Berin shook his hand.

"I'm very sorry that you're having to go through this. I wanted to let you know where we stand at the moment. Do you mind if we sit and talk?"

Berin only nodded once toward a pair of chairs near the corner of the room. As they started for them, Frank went for a walk.

Sitting and opening a manila file folder, Sergeant Tate said, "Employees at the airport confirm that your wife's flight arrived and that she was met by a driver that Forum identified as Emile Rees. Rees has a wife and three children, no criminal record, and has presumably never met your wife. While we are certainly not ruling out that he could've played a role in this, we are pursuing this as two missing persons."

Berin kept his gaze on the ground, taking in every word Tate said, but his emotions since hearing "your wife is missing" on the phone earlier were paralyzed in a state of dread.

"Our team investigated every property between here and Black Lake First Nations reservation. Based on interviews in Black Lake, there's no evidence showing that they ever made it there. There's no sign of the vehicle, an orange International Harvester Scout. However, we're not giving up. Tomorrow, we'll continue the search and focus on the land east of Highway 964." He closed the file and looked up at Berin, who was staring at the floor.

"Mr. van Tighem?"

No response.

"Mr. van Tighem!"

This time, Berin shifted his gaze slowly until it met Sergeant Tate's blue eyes.

"Thank you, Sergeant Tate." The words left his mouth with the force and depth that might come from a skeleton, if a skeleton could talk. And then Berin stood and walked slowly away.

That night, Berin did not speak to anyone except Frank, to whom he only said, "Good night." But in the morning, he knocked on Frank's door at 7:10 a.m. and said, "I'm walking the full stretch of 964 today. You don't have to come with me. I can meet you in Black Lake tonight."

"I'll come," he said. "Just give me a second to get changed."

In the lobby, Berin and Frank were met by Sergeant Tate.

"We're taking the Squirrel up in about twenty minutes. You're welcome to join us."

Frank responded, "I think we're going to—"

"Actually," Berin said, "maybe you should go with them."

"Berin—"

"If they find something, I want one of us to be there when they do." He gripped his brother's arm. "Do you understand?"

It was the first time Frank had seen this expression on his brother, the first time he had heard that defining tone.

He did understand, and his expression showed Berin that words were not needed.

The distance between Stony Rapids and the Black Lake Denesuline First Nation was about twenty kilometers. Very few people live along that stretch of road, so Berin would be on his own, but he needed that right now. After the first thirty minutes of walking, Stony Rapids out of sight, he slowed his pace and let the shock of the news finally pass through him so that he could focus.

Giant black spruce trees towered over the brown, dirt-packed highway letting only minor slivers of sunlight through the thicket. With each step, he felt that he was leaving one dimension and entering another, one where the wind did not breathe and where nothing lived beyond the veil of those trees because the only sound he could hear was his own footsteps. It was surreal. Dead silence, as if the woodland gods gave the command to assess this interloper.

It only lasted a few minutes, and then a breeze, and then the sound of wildlife returned.

Where was she? What had happened? Murders and kidnappings were not common anywhere in this region. And if it was something like that, surely there'd be at least one tiny piece of evidence. Berin kept walking. But there was nothing, just trees and bushes, wildlife and road. Just clouds and the heavens overhead. What about the driver? Ugh! None of it made sense. There were no motives. It was just a mystery.

As he continued, the landscape remained unchanging as if lost in a fairy's labyrinth. Berin became unsure of how far he'd traveled, what time it was, and even if he was still on the correct road. But, he kept on, shoes brown from the dirt, throat dry from neglect. Berin didn't let it slow him down. He marched on.

With Julia, he had no regrets. Yes, he had followed her everywhere, had given up any permanent career to remain mobile. But it had all been worth it, for she was the love of his life, he knew. Could he accept this if she was gone forever? Accept that she, his soulmate, would only be with him for a decade, and then she'd be gone forever? And he would suffer and grieve forever. He tried, oh, god, he tried not to think about what forever really meant. It was too overwhelming to feel that he'd never reach that level of happiness again. And it led him to the only certainty he'd had since it all began, that he wouldn't be able to accept that she was gone and would therefore never give up hope.

Berin had to clear his mind so that he could focus on any possible clues along the way. And for the next few kilometers, he was able to concentrate on his steps and then his breathing and the road. This worked for a while, it worked until he reached the halfway point between Stony Rapids and Black Lake where

THE THING IN THE WIND

Highway 964 curved to the east before becoming straight again. It was here that Berin's focus deteriorated. He stopped walking. He eyed the tops of spruce and hemlock and then spun slowly all the way around, all 360 degrees. When he leveled his head, staring down that straight rocky highway, he bellowed out her name: "Juliiiiaaaaa!"

When he ran out of breath, he took in air so deep his lungs felt as though they'd burst before howling out again: "Juuuuliiiiiiaaaaaa!"

Deep breath.

"Juuuuliiiiiiaaaaa!"

Another deep breath.

"Ahhhhhhhhhhh!"

Tears. Sobbing. Stifled breath.

"Juuliiiaaa! Please! Juliiaaaaaaa!"

Sinuses draining. Eyes draining. Breathing short and spasmodic.

He fell to his knees, his head bowed, and Berin van Tighem sobbed. He sobbed the way babies do—mouth agape screaming, face full of tears and snot, skin red as a devil's, and eyes mashed shut in agony. It was the kind of wailing one only does when someone has been taken too soon and without warning. The kind that one can only do when alone, for the weight and depth of the agony can only be expressed in solitude. He remained there on his knees for twenty full minutes, wailing, screaming out her name, and wailing some more until it died down to a whimper, and Berin's strength finally ceased. He lay back, staring up at the heavens, the stars of Draco, guardian of the Hesperides, staring back at him.

Berin remained there for an hour. That's how long it took for his tears to dry up and his strength to come back enough to get to his feet. With one heavy step at a time, he pushed on toward Black Lake.

At his slow pace, it took him almost three hours to get there. Frank and the helicopter crew had arrived several hours earlier and met him when he arrived.

"Jesus Christ, Berin!" said Frank. "You look like a zombie."

"Did you find anything?" Berin asked, his voice low and ragged, throat burning.

"No. Sorry." It was Sergeant Tate that had spoken up.

"I think we need to get you some food and water," said Frank.

"I'm not hungry, Frank." Berin's tone and expression were emotionless. He accepted the bottle of water Frank had for him, but he didn't open it. Instead, he endured what felt like needles scraping his inflamed throat.

"Sir," came a voice from behind Berin.

Berin turned around, but he didn't speak.

A man in a gray business suit said, "Sir, I'd like to speak to you in private, if you'd give a few minutes of your time."

The man was Berin's height, his skin tone and accent showing that he was part of the First Nations here in Black Lake. There was kindness in his brown eyes.

Without speaking, Berin took a few steps in the man's direction, and the man turned and led him to a small house no more than fifty feet away. Inside, the house was sparse, a minimalist's dream.

"Please, sit with me."

They sat in the front room. The walls were painted white and did not have any pictures or artwork hanging on them. The floors were wood, no stain or polyurethane, just thick boards that Berin presumed were freshly cut from the surrounding forest because the room itself smelled of the wilderness. In the middle of the room was a small bare table with four chairs surrounding it, where they sat.

"Can I offer you something to drink? Maybe marshmallow root with chamomile and lemon?"

"No, thank you."

He nodded. "I'm very sorry for your circumstances. We're all sorry." He spoke slowly, as if being sure to choose every word carefully. "I'm going to tell you something that goes against my tribe's wishes. We don't usually open up to outsiders, but I've determined that this situation should allow for a unique circumstance. And I base that on the circumstances of your wife and her driver's disappearance."

Berin could feel his heart pounding the back of his chest, could feel it in his arms and just behind his ears. Was this hope? Did this man know something?

"It's possible," the man continued, "that there's something else at work here. Something that you will probably scoff at, will probably not believe. And that's okay. But know that it is all I can tell you, so please don't ask me any questions or ask for more clarification. Are we agreed?"

Berin could see the sincerity in this man's eyes. He somehow knew that what this man was about to say would be more important than anything he uncovered, anything the Mounties uncovered, or anything anyone else could uncover, so he simply nodded once in agreement.

"Okay," the man said. Taking in a deep breath, he said, "The Dene have certain beliefs not associated with what the white man brought over from Europe. One of those beliefs is in a spirit, more precisely a creature that is sometimes called the protector of the wilderness. Sometimes the call of the wild. And, in certain darker cases, synonymous with one of our species' most horrible acts: cannibalism. It's a dark spirit, often tied in with famine or possibly some kind of impending doom. We call it the wendigo." The man leaned forward. "These creatures have the power to sour a land and sour a mind. And those it takes, well, they can turn them into wendigos as well. I fear that if you see your wife again, it won't really be her any longer." The man stood, maintaining eye contact with Berin.

Berin sat silently for several seconds, taking in what the man had said. It wasn't what he had hoped, but the idea that he would be able to see her again resonated and lingered.

"That's all I can really tell you. Nothing else would be helpful, other than the hope that I'm wrong." The man stood slowly. "There are books, of course, if you want to know more."

Berin stood and extended his hand. When the man took it, Berin said, "I'm only interested in her. Thank you for trusting me and talking to me about this. I know it's not the typical thing to do, so it means a lot."

"My pleasure."

Releasing the man's hand, Berin asked, "You haven't told me your name. Do you mind?"

He smiled. "Robillard. I am the chief here."

"Berin," he replied. "Chief Robillard, I know that you said no questions, but I do have one that I hope you can answer." Without waiting for a response, he asked, "If it is true and there is a wendigo out there, how would I know?"

Robillard's smile disappeared. "You would know because you will feel like you are being hunted."

V

After a full week of searching, the RCMP did not uncover one shred of evidence. Orders were received from Saskatoon for the extra officers they had sent up to return because they had to use their resources elsewhere, leaving the local police to handle it and leaving Berin without a wife and without hope. It crippled him. The only reason why he didn't get on a boat, tie a rock to his feet, and become one with Lake Athabasca was Frank. Berin wasn't playing the father role anymore, but Frank needed him.

While Frank was younger, he was able to see this particular situation with far more clarity than Berin. His method was to pull his brother into work to help ease his obsessed mind. Berin wanted to stay in either Black Lake or Stony Rapids so that he could continue searching on his own, staying in the last place his Julia had been.

"I can't give up, Frank!"

"I'm not asking you to," Frank said. "I just want you to come back to Fort Chip with me. We'd only be an hour's plane ride away from here if they find anything. You're not doing anyone any good just sitting here and waiting."

Berin knew that his brother was right, so he stood up and let Frank take him back across the lake.

They fixed up the boat they'd bought. Frank linked up with a woman named Michelle in Edmonton who knew how to make a strong website and manage it, and the brothers became part of the tourism industry, taking terrible fishermen out onto Lake Athabasca, giving them fishing poles and bait, and sitting back while they tried to snag a trout or walleye. Whether they were successful or not, the brothers got paid, along with Michelle back in Edmonton. While their initial discussion with Athabasca Fishing Tours had seemed promising, the company went out of business a few months afterwards when two more of their boats broke down and the costs for repair were too much, making their boat the only one for anglers out of Fort Chipewyan.

Berin slowly gave the outward appearance that he was okay, but Frank knew that he wasn't, and he also knew that there was nothing he could do about it. Forum told Berin that he could keep the house for a year, which he did; however, afterwards, when Julia had been considered deceased, a funeral had been performed, and a death certificate had been issued, Berin found a very inexpensive place in a settlement on the northern shore of Lake Athabasca, Camsell Portage, and decided to move there. Frank went with him, feeling as though he owed Berin a minimum of two years for the time he'd played the role of father. But, he would have joined him regardless because he loved his brother. Besides, it wasn't as if he had anything or anyone causing him to question such a decision. With the two of them in Camsell Portage, it raised the population from thirty-seven to thirty-nine.

While in Camsell Portage, they simply existed. Frank would take on the occasional high-paying anglers out of Fort Chip, but they were few and far between. Berin befriended an old reclusive man in a neighboring house that he'd visit a few times per week. Aside from those conversations, Berin would sit on the front porch gazing out at Nature or sit on the boat peering at the lake, as if having asked it a question and awaiting a much-anticipated answer. But, there was never an answer, just the sound of insects, birds, and the light lapping of water along the shoreline. It was during those times on the boat, looking out at the placid water, that he'd weep so hard he thought his stomach would tear open. Where was she? What happened out there? He knew that if he wanted answers to those questions, he'd have to find them on his own, but his will was broken, and he fell into a deeper depression.

Michelle, God bless her, had kept up the website. While she would usually send an e-mail when a regular job came along, this request was different. The man was not a tourist or weekend fisherman; he was going to be there for an entirely different reason, so Michelle picked up her cell phone and called. When Berin answered and she explained the man's request, Berin changed from a cold shell of a man to one who had a fire ignited within him. After accepting the job, Frank felt somewhat confused, but, as always, went along with it. If a guy wanted to pay to be chauffeured across the lake, then fine. And if he wanted to pay such an absurd rate, then great, whether they needed the money or not. It'd be an adventure. A change. For Berin, it was a sign.

CHAPTER 3:
GUINEVERE WALTER

i

GUINEVERE WALTER HADN'T expected to move to Yellowknife, the capital of the Northwest Territories, and fall in love with the place, but that's precisely what she did after her husband, Jacob Blacktree, was offered a position at DeBeers. Guin stood slightly under six feet tall, bookworm thin, with dark wavy hair that she kept pulled back in a ponytail half the time. She'd moved often in her life, never able to consider a place permanent, but when they drove the rental car from Yellowknife Airport to their new house (the outside looking like a large log cabin, but the inside like a cookie-cutter home she was used to back in Denver . . . the walls a textured sheetrock rather than wood or plaster over lathing) just off School Draw Road, she got out, walked to the backyard where there was a dock stretching out into Great Slave Lake, and stared out at the water for nearly ten minutes. *This is my home,* she thought. *This is* my *home. My home.* She knew before stepping foot inside the cabin that she didn't want to leave this place, that it would be her last move. Over the following month, as if her thoughts had manifested and solidified it, she'd found employment at Aurora College teaching environmental studies, tiptoeing in her mother's footsteps. That was two years ago.

It was late October, dusk, and Guin stood gazing at the sheet of black glass that was Great Slave Lake. The water reflected a crescent moon amid sparse clouds drifting east at a snail's pace as the howling of hungry gray wolves shimmered across the water and settled in her ears, hypnotic like the tones from a Tibetan sound bowl. She came out here every evening and waited for a long day to dim or a short day to turn black and stay that way for a while. It hadn't taken her long to grow accustomed to the north—just one year—unlike many others who usually suffered from insomnia half the year because the sun refused to say good night and depression the other half from long stretches of darkness, but not her. Overlooking the lake, her only witness the vast and misty pine forest, Guin usually dumped her grief into her journal in a controlled, meticulous manner: one minor memory at a time. But tonight was different—tonight, the dam that regulated those memories had ruptured, and the effects showed in her shaky hands, chewed bottom lip, and makeup-streaked cheeks from thirty minutes' worth of tears. She wished the reflection of the late October sky held a full moon, wished the air was crisp like a York apple, but it was heavy, not the dry air she'd gotten used to back in Denver, but the humid cold that found its way to your bones. It was York apples that she and her parents picked at the Armstrong Orchard so long ago in Virginia. Some to eat, some to use in apple pies, and some to go in fruit baskets for the neighbors on Thanksgiving. She'd always sneak a few and stash them in her bedroom, unable to resist their tartness and sweet aftertaste. She favored those even more than the candy she collected on Halloween in Jefferson, Virginia—the farthest her family could get from the Pentagon, where her father spent most of his waking hours five or six days per week. It was the Jefferson memories that made this evening different, brought on by the phone conversation with her father just two hours ago. Memories flooded her mind, too many to jot down in her leather-bound journal.

She'd started writing because of her mother, Shirley. At the young age of ten, Guin was helping unpack boxes in their new home in Jefferson, and she'd found several notebooks full of her mother's thoughts, hopes, dreams, and nightmares. The family history. Her mother's childhood, a house with a set of parents that quoted scripture by day and seemed in league with the devil by night—arguing and drinking and arguing some more until it got violent. That's when Shirley would run to her hideaway in the copse of trees between her house and the neighboring sub-division, an immense forest from her perspective. A place for solace. A place that never caused her harm. And, later, a place where she would meet her secret boyfriend, where that secret boyfriend would take her virginity, and where the city of Knoxville, Tennessee, would build a four-lane road two months before she left for college, sealing beneath the thick macadam the only patch of land Shirley could ever label sacred. With her scholarship to the University of Washington, she took a Greyhound bus to Seattle and never stepped foot in Tennessee again. Guin had noticed a distinct shift in the entries once her mother had reached Seattle. Aside from constant nightmares, the entries would have been quite boring to anyone but Guin. Shirley had met Guin's father, Eugene, her junior year. They'd fallen in love, and the rest was history. It was a lot for a ten-year-old to process, much of which she did not understand until later in life. Some of which she didn't understand now. Especially the nightmares, something she had inherited from her mother. From what she remembered from the journals, the nightmare Guin had been having for the past week was similar to one her mother wrote about more than once. In her mother's version, Shirley was herself, watching it all unfold as if viewing a film, but Guin's had the perspective of an adolescent boy.

The reverie was broken by the sound of hollow footsteps, Guin's liquid reflection staring back at her.

"Everything okay?" asked Jacob. He kept his distance, knowing that her time on the dock at night was important to her; it was *her* time. But the temperature had grown colder, and he used it as an excuse to check on her. "It's been almost an hour."

"I'm fine, honey." She kept her voice steady and her back to him. "I'll be inside soon."

"Here you go." He put a throw blanket around her shoulders, then, with a nod that she did not see and an "okay" that she did not respond to, went back inside.

The Jefferson Journals, she'd coined them, were filled with good memories like those at the Armstrong Orchard. Nightmares, yes, but the repetition of such entries caused her to grow desensitized, and she eventually stopped sneaking into her parents' bedroom to read her mother's journals; after all, she was there, living most of it. The earlier tomes that had demanded her attention were written about a time before she was born, filled with people she'd never met or knew existed.

If her family had remained in Jefferson, she thought, it would have been perfect, but her father's military career yanked her away from her friends and school every four years. After high school graduation, Guin decided to stay in Denver to attend college rather than following her parents to San Antonio. In that time, she'd gotten her B.S. in Environmental Studies at the University of Denver, then her master's at Colorado University in Boulder, gotten married, and settled in the small and isolated community of Yellowknife, choosing harsh winters with Jacob Blacktree, her anchor, rather than her high school sweetheart, Anton Thames, who had been accepted into the Air Force Academy in Colorado Springs, a man on his way to becoming like her father, the trailblazer. And she was happy with her decision. Jacob and Yellowknife gave her a chance for the peace and stability she'd yearned for growing up . . . at least she wanted to believe that. Even though she'd stopped reading her mother's journals back in Jefferson, she'd known that they were available should she want to delve into her mother's mind again. But that changed when her parents left for Texas and she stayed in Colorado. It was that very night that she'd begun inking her life onto the page, carrying on a tradition. Did her mother ever know that she'd read her journals? Guin didn't know.

If only her mind was as placid as the lake, but the conversation she'd had with her father was shocking. For the first time in her life, she'd heard her father's voice quiver and almost break as if he had been holding back tears, keeping that lump from seizing his throat. "Shirley's dead," he'd said. "Your mother's dead."

It wasn't late, just 5:30 p.m., but Guin was exhausted. The temperature had dropped even more as thick clouds moved in, covering the stars and moon. The first few flurries had fallen by the time she reached the back door. Inside, the temperature was much warmer. She slipped off the throw Jacob had brought her, then her coat, then tied the leather strap around her journal. That was another gift the lake had given her—she could open up and give it all of her thoughts, her grief, her tears, and she could move on with the rest of her night until the following evening . . . her way of keeping Jacob at a distance when she had to.

"Hun?" said Jacob.

"Yeah," she responded, gazing down the long, carpeted hallway that ended at the kitchen. The dim light given off from the kitchen's fluorescent bulbs outlined the only two items hanging on the wall: her and Jacob's wedding photo on the right wall; a picture of seventeen-year-old Jacob and his family on the left. She'd worn a white dress that draped down to her ankles, her black hair resting on her shoulders, and, at her insistence with the maid of honor, her black-rimmed glasses, the same ones she wore tonight. And Jacob, his deep-set brown eyes locked with hers, a goofy smile spread across his face. It was the same one he'd worn after she'd agreed to marry him on a night almost as cold as this one before bathing in the steamy Glenwood Springs in Colorado.

"Can you come into the kitchen?"

Guin wiped her face before rounding the corner to the scent of cooking fish in the room. "What's all this?" She saw giant cocktail shrimp in a glass bowl, cocktail sauce, filets of baked fish—she didn't know what kind—on a plate, the steam showing that it'd just been taken off the heat, and Jacob sautéing scallops. It helped get her mind off the memories, but they were still lingering. She didn't have an appetite, but a stirring in her gut made her feel almost ravenous, that urge to consume.

"Just thought you might like something . . . special," he said, glancing back at her with a smile, then returned his eyes to the scallops. "There's also a bottle of chardonnay if you're in the mood."

She knew that he'd do something like this. Work at the mine had kept him away for long hours, and sometimes he had to sleep at his office. He'd told her that he hated leaving her for so long, especially near or during winter, when the days were short and the weather less than tolerable. The environment had a way of spreading misery during its long spells of darkness. Here, people had to be close enough to Nature to understand Her. To coexist. And this feeling like he should do something special for Guin, she knew, didn't come from her complaining about him being gone or blaming him for taking her to the middle of nowhere, for she never spoke a word of it or showed signs that it bothered her. She had adapted to it all much more quickly than he had; moreover, she needed it. The only change that had ever satisfied her craving for stability. So, she acted surprised at the seafood dinner and wine for his sake because she also knew that he hadn't adapted at all and that this special dinner was more for him than for her. *I guess I'm the anchor.* Guin also had to hide her disinterest in eating. Under the circumstances, it didn't matter what he had cooked, her mind was elsewhere.

"Chardonnay sounds good," she said calmly, opening the chilled bottle.

THE THING IN THE WIND

Jacob wasted little time getting the remaining food on the table.

"So, you just felt like doing something special?" she said.

She watched him sit down. He was only twenty-nine and his hair was thinning, the puffiness under his eyes slightly purple and red, and a few early wrinkles had formed near his mouth as if he was a smoker, but, to her knowledge, he hadn't smoked a day in his life.

"It's been a hard couple of months. I told Andy that I—"

"Who's Andy again?" She was only half listening, her attention shifting from his somewhat haggard appearance to the food.

"You haven't met him. He was a manager at one of the African mines, and now he's my new boss. But I told him that I couldn't keep working so many hours of overtime like he's been asking me to do. I mean, they've had me going from Snap Lake to Gahcho Kué and back again. It's absurd." He didn't take his eyes off her. "I don't think it's fair to you for me to be gone all the time."

Guin gave a quick smile, then said, "Don't do it on account of me. I understand that you have work; I understood how it'd be before we got married." She dipped a shrimp in the cocktail sauce, then bit it in half. It was overcooked, but she didn't care. Chewing the rubbery crustacean felt satisfying, necessary. It felt good to be chewing something, tasting the heat and bitterness of the cocktail sauce, to hear the ripping sound as her teeth tore through the shrimp's body . . . It made her think of the wolves she'd heard howling near the lake. It made her mind shift from the phone call with her father.

He brought up work often, so she tried to keep the conversation as light as possible. Part of her felt sorry for Jacob. She was his partner, but she knew that she was putting herself first this time, that no matter how badly he wanted to leave, to move to a warmer and more populated place, she'd refuse. And she'd had enough moving in her life. She wouldn't let him take her away from her lake, her dock, her home.

"I just worry that you—"

"I am fine," she said slowly, then swallowed the chewed shrimp. "I have my work and my hobbies." And that was true—she enjoyed the lake, her students, and their friends. She enjoyed Old Town and seeing the Aurora Borealis regularly. She loved the bright green grass in the warm months and the dark evergreens during winter. To her, Yellowknife was the top of the world, and she intended to stay there. Yellowknife was to her what that copse . . . no, that sanctuary of trees and oak-tree altar had been for her mother, but Guin would not simply go along quietly if anyone threatened to take her Yellowknife away. They'd talked about this subject in the past. It had never turned into an argument, but it had gotten close once. About a year ago, just after Jacob had gotten a generous raise, he came home after being away for three days at the mine. He was angry because he'd had to fire a friend of his, corporate's orders. "As if the dark days weren't bad enough," he'd yelled, "now I have to live with this! What's his family going to do now? I wouldn't be surprised if they didn't have any savings. And I can't just forget about him; he's my friend, for God's sake! I never should've taken this fucking job and moved us all the way up to Nowhere, Canada, where most of the people are in poverty and the fucking temperature doesn't even get up to zero most of the year." She let him get it all out, hoping he wouldn't want to move. If so, that would've been their first *real* fight.

Guin cut a large scallop in half, put it in her mouth, then said, "Mmm. You cooked these perfectly." Unlike the shrimp, the scallop practically melted in her mouth and slid down her throat. It was one way to keep her mind occupied, even if only for a few minutes.

Jacob wasn't a violent man, but his outburst on the night he had fired his friend had shown her a different side of him, one that she hadn't seen before . . . or since. Maybe it wouldn't be so bad to move, she thought, if it made him happy. The only problem was being sure the next place would be home . . . or the next. She didn't want to keep going in circles: moving, making new friends, building a home that was comfortable, finding a job that she liked, only to move again and start the cycle over. It reminded her of a song that she and some of her schoolmates sang at recess when she was a child: "Ring around the Rosie, a pocketful of posies, ashes, ashes, we all fall down." She had found out the tune's meaning much earlier than her friends. The morbid children's game wasn't fun at all. When she mentioned it to her teacher, Mrs. Jewels, she received a pat on the head and a "quite analytical, my dear" before being told to get her backpack and not miss the bus home. That was the moment she learned to keep certain things to herself . . . like mentioning the conversation she'd had with her father. She'd have to tell Jacob eventually, but not now.

THE THING IN THE WIND

Jacob nodded, then said, "Thanks." Letting out a deep breath, he said, "You're sure my work schedule doesn't bother you—"

"Promise," she said, feeling the annoyance slither up her spine. "I like our life here. And I like more that you can move up very quickly in your job here." She took a sip of wine, keeping her appearance calm but working hard to hide her frustration at the repetition of this kind of discussion. "Now eat before it gets cold." That was her fear: not having any permanence in the world. Never having a place to really call home, a place that gave her the peace and solace that this almost forgotten place gave her. She wasn't a trailblazer like her father and didn't want to be. Without a home to go back to, life was nomadic and had no real purpose. Without it, she thought, she may as well fall down.

The oven alarm startled her.

"I almost forgot," said Jacob, "dessert." He smiled. "Apple pie."

ii

Guin woke to an empty bed. Outside the window, the thermometer read 12 degrees Fahrenheit. In a month, the high wouldn't exceed -10. *I've got to learn Celsius like the rest of the world.* After showering and dressing, Guin took a small wooden box out of her closet and unlocked it. Inside were eight pictures of her parents in various places—San Antonio, Galveston, San Diego, and Anchorage, where her father's most recent post had been. Under a loaded derringer, a stack of letters that she'd read countless times lay dormant. She hadn't opened the box in nearly six months, when the last letter had been received, along with the photo of her parents on a hike, a moose far in the background drinking from the creek.

It hadn't taken her father long to regain his composure. "She and two colleagues met in Fort Resolution," he'd said, "trying to help out the locals between there and Black Lake. Apparently, the tar sands are causing some pretty horrible conditions in the Athabasca region, not so different from what the mountaintop removal activists were arguing back in Virginia, just on a much bigger scale. They traveled from Fort Res all the way to Stony Rapids, taking water and soil samples and conducting interviews along the way. Said it was the last chance they'd have before winter, so they rushed. They didn't make it to Black Lake. My last contact with her . . . " He'd paused here, leaving the hum of the line to fill in the silence. " . . . was when they got to Stony Rapids. That was two weeks ago. She told me that she'd planned to surprise you with a visit once they'd finished up. Then, a week later, I got a call from Canadian authorities, and they told me that she was dead and they'd airlifted her to Saskatoon. I don't even want to get into the difficulties of what someone must do if a spouse dies abroad. But, I'm in Saskatoon now."

"What happened, Dad? Do they know?" It had been all she could think to say. It hadn't seemed real. Not the news, not the circumstances, not even her father's voice, for she hadn't heard it in nearly a year.

"They don't." He paused again. "Guin, honey, the details are . . . " This was where he choked up again. "They didn't . . . I couldn't . . . I'm not able to see her yet. She wanted to be cremated, so I'm having her cremated. No service. You know how your mom felt about those sorts of things."

She had known. Of all the people she'd met, her mother was the only one to dismiss all things supernatural, whether it be Old Saint Nick or Krampus, ghosts in the graveyard or zombies, or even God or the Devil, it didn't matter. What did matter was science and evidence, or theories built upon such practices. However, she did take much delight in reading about such absurdities as haunted houses, demonic possessions, or monsters lurking in the shadows . . . maybe because of the dreams that haunted her most nights.

Much of this kind of thinking had been passed on to Guin; however, she kept the door open to the possibility of the supernatural. Her dreams were too vivid and profound for her to do otherwise. While she was awake, the natural world, especially when gazing up into the cosmos, was wondrous and sublime enough to keep her imagination from probing too deep into the fantastical. How insignificant she felt when considering all that was out there in the great beyond, and how it made so many problems surrounding her seem inconsequential. Maybe that was why she didn't want to move again. The stresses of life getting in the way of trying to comprehend and understand her place in the universe. And what better place to contemplate such inquiries as in Yellowknife, her top of the world?

"Did they tell you anything more?" she said.

"Not much, honey. According to Edmund, the one that

survived, he said that three people went into the backwoods, and that two of them died. Edmund was cleared of any wrongdoing. After searching for Annalisa for five days, they gave up the search. They think animals got to her. I'm going to talk to Edmund, then retrace her steps," he'd said. "It's just something I have to do."

Silence.

"I want you to come with me, Guin."

Without pause, she'd replied, "Okay."

The end of the call had been abrupt, and she had gone about her day, teaching two classes, then returning home to the dock, where she tried letting what had happened sink in.

Putting the photos and letters back in the box, and slipping the box back on a closet shelf, Guin then put her black hair in a ponytail, washed her face, and put on a few extra layers before taking the eight-minute walk to the Wildcat Café.

The bell above the door chimed as she made her way inside, the hearty scent of caribou stew in the air. The owner, Agnes, was giving a customer change before noticing Guin. When she looked at Agnes' green eyes, she could tell that it had been a long night. Agnes usually seemed as if she'd had a pot of her own oil-thick coffee every morning Guin saw her, but this morning was much different. Her bright eyes were dim and her tall, petite frame held the posture of an elderly woman.

Guin rested her elbows on the counter and asked, "Is the baby still waking up every two hours?" The thought of Agnes having had the child just five months ago and having already lost all the weight perplexed her.

"It's every hour, and I need some coffee. Been an odd morning. I didn't want to say anything to you with that man here . . . he's part of what's odd." She poured two cups of coffee and motioned for Guin to sit with her. "Have you noticed anything strange?"

She took a sip of the steamy coffee, noticing Agnes' look of relief once she had gotten off her feet. "No, I can't say that I have." For Agnes to feel that something was odd got under Guin's skin. Her friend was not the kind to gossip or buy into superstition. If she broke a mirror, she cleaned up the mess and bought a new one. If gossip began, she changed the subject to something meaningful like her daughter's latest feat, which she'd go on and on about until the gossiper took the hint and shut up.

"And Jacob?"

"No." She looked around the empty restaurant. "The only oddity is that you're not busy this morning."

The Wildcat Café had been in Yellowknife for many decades, and the locals and tourists alike made it a point to visit regularly. Agnes' grandmother had handed it down to her mother, who had passed away seven years ago from pneumonia, and she'd passed it down to Agnes, knowing that she would be responsible and not sell it or let it depreciate. In fact, since Agnes had taken ownership, business had increased steadily each year. Her college work in business management had emphasized advertising, so she focused her effort on the internet, making sure to highlight their unique menu and history. It was something Guin always admired in her. The idea of stability and, more importantly, the idea of a real home. Agnes had attended college in Ottawa and could have done anything, but she chose her hometown, Yellowknife, to come back to, even when her mother was still alive. Agnes was thirty-four, and Guin had no doubt that in thirty-four more years her friend would still be in Yellowknife running the Wildcat. That was something to envy.

"It's not so much *that* as it is people just not talking. The guy in here a few minutes ago works at the airport. Comes in about three mornings a week and chats it up with Leon, but not today. And there's been several come in that just aren't talking."

"Well, you know how some people start to get around this time of year. Just be glad they're drinking coffee . . . " As she took another sip, she heard the radio newsman announce that a snowstorm would pass through the region later tonight. No matter how often they blew through, she never tired of gazing out the window at the falling snow as each snowflake danced down from the lonely sky and weaved itself into a white blanket. That's how she described it anyway.

"I'm just glad you're not that way."

Guin smiled, then glanced toward the register. "Is she back in the office?"

"Yeah, Leon's back there taking care of her." She stared at her reflection in the smoky coffee. "And that's odd, too. She's been quiet since we got here this morning." Agnes stood up and started laughing. "I'm probably losing it, eh? They say that happens when you don't get much sleep." Back to the counter, she said, "Teaching this afternoon?"

"Yeah. Just two more weeks before the break. And none of them better have this silent spell!"

"That'll be good," she said. "Breaks are very good."

She was looking forward to winter break, but Guin knew what Agnes was really referring to, and it had nothing to do with her environmental studies courses at Aurora College. She still hadn't heard a sound from the back room . . .

Guin's thoughts turned to her class. Her students, she thought, had taught her more in two years than her professors had in six. She was so fascinated by Algonquin folklore and Northern lifestyle that her course often turned into a literature class or seminar in Inuit culture, and she had to force herself to shift back to the environment. But, she would always be a student at heart, learning whatever snagged just a bit of her interest. She'd always been that way. Just before harvest in Jefferson, she'd listened to Victor Armstrong talk about the different apples growing in his family's orchards. And she remembered her mother supporting her wanting to have an orchard of her own and letting her plant three apple trees in their modest backyard. Her mother had shown her a passage from Ovid's *Metamorphosis* after Guin had dressed as the Roman goddess Pomona that Halloween. And Guin memorized the passage from that work:

Pomona lived, when Procas, next in line,
Reigned o'er the people of the Palatine.
She tended orchards, and in care of trees
Was first among the woodland deities.
No Latian rival could surpass her pride
In fruit-tree culture—as her name implied.

It wasn't until she was older that she realized why her mother had been hesitant at first, making sure to reiterate to her that trees took a long time to grow and mature before being able to bear fruit, knowing that Guin would never see the first apple ready to be picked from those trees. It was the military way—as soon as roots attempted to settle, they were ripped from the ground and transplanted somewhere across the country to a place with different soil, a different climate, and different expectations; at least that's how Guin saw it.

She whispered the passage to herself in the Wildcat Café, smiling over her warm mug of coffee. Her dream of an apple orchard hadn't faded away. There was something special about those trees, those rows and rows of trees stretching on for what seemed like miles, all bearing fruit, all full of life, all firmly rooted in thick, fertile soil. But there was something special about the North Country, too. Whatever it was, it gave her peace. There was no fear in its cold and endless forests or its muggy bogs. There was no anxiety from the wolves howling in the dusk or loons crying in the night. It made her feel safe and rooted, like those trees at Victor Armstrong's orchard. Maybe that was why Agnes' worry about silence didn't worry her. To an outsider, the North Country was full of sound, the music of Nature constantly humming in the thicket, a chorus hidden just beyond the tree line. To the native, the singing was a peaceful silence.

iii

At twilight, blustery wind agitated the lake, shoving cold waves higher on the bank than Guin had ever remembered. Splashes of water even soaked the dock, making it slippery as stinging gales turned it to ice. And the lake would be ice soon, insulating itself from the long and dark winter ahead. She felt as if she'd been doing the same, insulating herself not with ice, but with time and distance.

Her thoughts were repetitive: Yellowknife had a way of making the rest of the world inconsequential, giving her solace in the never-ending taiga and mossy bogs where few traveled. At times when Jacob would be away for days, she'd pack the tent and venture into the woods with little food, a fishing pole, and her journal. She was ready to go there now, into the solitude, and let Nature be her companion—Nature was her true home, she thought. Not the Old Town house with the dock, but the natural elements surrounding the entire town.

"It's beautiful here, isn't it?"

She hadn't heard that voice in—"Dad!" She turned around and there he was, Colonel Eugene Walter, standing at the dock entrance, face as dignified as the silver eagles pinned to his epaulets. The worry vanished as she ran into his open arms. She was his little girl again. "I didn't expect you so soon." When she felt his arms around her, the grief finally surfaced, the truth clear. Her mother was gone. It was real. Even if it hadn't shown on his face, she felt his grief and sadness, for he held her more tightly than he ever had, arms tense and stony, stinking of exhaustion.

THE THING IN THE WIND

There was something about her father's smile that didn't seem right, she thought. It was because he never smiled! There had to be something that she didn't know, something he was keeping from her. "It's been so long. All I have are pictures and letters you've sent me."

"I know—"

"I'm just glad you're here." And that was true. They weren't just words. If his smile was for seeing her again and that was it, then so be it. She was honored. But, everything was odd today. Nobody speaking at the Wildcat, her students not saying much in class that afternoon, and now her father showing up so soon with a huge smile on his face. Nothing made sense. Did he have other news about her mother? Had anything changed? Had she been cremated yesterday?

Inside, she saw her father more clearly: sleepless eyes, slumped shoulders, and deep-set wrinkles curving across his face. He was a haggard colonel, and she knew that his smile was merely an attempt to veil the pain that dwelled deep in his gut. It wasn't just her mother's death, she knew, but his entire life seemed to have caught up with him—Desert Storm, Libya, Grenada, Cold War, murdered parents; it was all scripted on his wrinkled face, in his bloodshot eyes. She realized that she was all he had left in the world that could be called family.

He turned and faced the wedding photo. "I retired, Guin," he said almost grimly.

She almost didn't believe she'd heard him correctly, that the cold air seeping in as she closed the back door had distorted the words. "Dad," she said in more of a whisper.

"It's what I needed, honey," he said, turning to face her. "That part of my life is over." He seemed to grit his teeth a moment before putting his arms out, palms up, and then smirking. "This is the last time you'll see me in a uniform, kid."

"I-I don't know what to say." She didn't move, just stared at him for a moment, shadows covering the top half of his face so that she could only see part of his nose and mouth, those exposed teeth reflecting the lamplight mournfully.

"Nothing *to* say." He approached her, took off his hat, and motioned for her to sit down on the couch.

The house was silent and gloomy. The springs in the sofa cushion squeaked like a door opening in a horror movie when they sat.

"I meant what I said on the phone. I want to retrace her steps, find out what really happened out there." He gripped the hat more firmly, the sound reverberating like grinding leather. "I'm not going to be able to rest until I do."

"And you want me with you."

"I want you with me." He sat back, exhaling as if he'd been holding his breath, then gazed up at the dim ceiling. "I've arranged everything. We can leave tomorrow. I don't know when we'll be back."

This was not like him. Yes, having everything scheduled and ready, but not a sudden change, especially without planning, without giving her the heads up.

"I should be able to get class coverage . . . "

"Good. And Jacob?"

Yes, Jacob. Now it would be her away from home for a time. How would he handle it? Probably not well, but it was what she had to do. "He'll be fine, Dad." She didn't really believe that. Where they'd be going, she'd not be accessible most of the way. Jacob was usually on-site where cell phones worked and there was internet, but she'd be in the wilderness, detached. Maybe he wouldn't be fine. "So, what is the plan?"

"We will fly to Hay River Airport and meet Edmund there, then fly to Fort Chipewyan. Boat across the *Lake of the Hills*—"

"Athabasca."

"Yes, to Stony Rapids. We're on snowmobile from there to Black Lake. Edmund will be taking us into the woods where it all happened." He shook his head as he continued. "They stopped the search for Annalisa, but Edmund is . . . I don't know . . . hopeful."

"There's no way that she could have survived out there for that long without the police finding her."

"That's not for me to judge, Guin. If we can help Edmund find closure at the same time I hope to, it'll be good."

She nodded. It sounded odd, but Guin understood. Edmund would serve as guide. The odd part was his willingness to go back there so soon after the tragedy. Guin didn't know if she would have the same kind of strength.

"So, we go to Black Lake, go to where this happened, and then what?" She wanted to hear him say it, to say how he'd get closure by being where it happened, whatever "it" had been.

He cleared his throat. "Your mother had been on hundreds of

these research teams, been in the field enough to feel at home when out there doing her work."

"Like you in the service."

"Exactly. I just don't know what happened. The doctors don't know. Edmund doesn't know. No one knows a damn thing." His gaze dropped to the floor. "It's the only thing I can do, Guin. The only place that might have an answer. I can't be one of those people that let months and years pass by without a solid answer or at least doing everything I can to get the answers available."

That would have to suffice because Guin couldn't bring herself to talk about it anymore. It was going to happen, and she could only hope for answers waiting for them out there in the wilderness. However, when he spoke again, some of those answers came, and they made her squirm.

"Guin . . . " He swallowed hard, like someone trying to swallow a pill without water, and looked at her with his tired and bloodshot eyes. "In Saskatoon, they only had a few bones."

Guin gasped! Tears that had been hiding began welling up as if on cue.

"They were found with her scarf and identification, which is why they think they belong to her."

She covered her nose and mouth with her hands reflexively, giving him a look that seemed to scream "Stop telling me this! I don't want to hear this!"

"So, at this point, it's possible that your mother's still alive or that she's still out there somewhere." He took in a deep breath, then added, "I thought that I was going to Saskatoon to identify her body and get questions answered, but I only have more questions now. For all I know, those bones belong to Annalisa."

Those initial tears and spikes of pain erupting within Guin shifted slightly at this hope.

"The odds are that she's gone, but I'm not ready to give up hope," he said. "And . . . " he choked up.

Guin nearly leapt toward him, throwing her arms around him and squeezing him as tightly as she could. "I love you, Daddy! I understand."

His arms wrapped around her, but he didn't squeeze with all his might; instead, tenderly and with care as she buried her face in his neck.

"I'll go with you the whole way," she said, her voice slightly muffled.

When Guin let him go a full two minutes later, she had regained composure and wiped the tears and snot from her face, then she nodded.

"I'll be by at eight in the morning to pick you up. All you'll need is a backpack with a few changes of clothes. I've arranged for everything else we'll need when we get there."

iv

Jacob got home an hour later. Guin sat in the kitchen looking out the window.

"Hey," he said. "I didn't expect you home."

She turned to him. He was in a suit and tie, folder tucked under his left arm, and he wore a smile that she erased very quickly when she said, "I need to talk to you."

He let the folder drop, then knelt in front of her, taking her hands in his. "You look distraught. What is it?"

"It's my mother," she began. It was the only part of the brief story in which she had to pause to prevent herself from crying again. But it only lasted a few seconds before she continued. As she spoke, Jacob didn't say a word, just gripped her hands as she told him the abridged version, leaving out the uncertain and gory details. "And, so, I leave tomorrow morning, and I don't know how long I'll be gone."

"Oh my god, Guin . . . I'm so sorry. Please tell me that there's something I can do."

She closed her eyes and shook her head.

"Why didn't you tell me yesterday?" he asked. "I feel bad about going on and on about work when you had this on your mind." He stood. "Please let me help. I can come with you."

"You have enough stress with work right now—"

"But *I* need to be here for *you*. I love you." He hugged her tightly. "I can't believe this happened. Are you really okay?"

"Yes," she said, slightly pushing him away, then putting her hands on his shoulders and staring him in the eyes. "I'm okay. And I'll be better when I get back."

Jacob nodded silently, shifting his gaze from her to the floor and back up to her again. "And when you get back, you're sure you want to stay here? It'll be winter soon, and you want to go through that again?" His words were choppy, like those of a child trying to talk while stifling a cry.

THE THING IN THE WIND

"There is no problem on my end. Our life here makes me happy, Jacob. I wouldn't want it any other way." She was growing frustrated, but she tried to keep it hidden.

Brows furrowing, Jacob looked as if he was about to cry. "Are you serious?"

"I don't know how many more ways I can say it or how many more times."

Tongue pressing against his upper lip and a quick nod, Jacob let out an "okay" before standing up. "I don't know how I feel here."

There it was . . . the words she feared would make it out of his mouth. There were a few choices that she could make. She could be more firm and tell him that she wasn't moving under any circumstances and that he'd have to deal with it or find another wife. She could sympathize and get into a long discussion about it. Or, she could use the tragedy in her favor and tell him that it's something she can't talk about right now, not with the current situation with her mother. And that's what she chose, knowing the first choice was far too harsh and that she didn't have time or mental energy for the second.

"Of course. Sorry. I just—"

"It's okay. It's just taking you longer to adjust. But you will. And when you do, you'll be happy."

Nodding, he said, "Hope so." Then, he leaned in and kissed her.

Guin received the kiss, but there was a feeling of frustration zipping through her rather than love, a feeling that connected her more strongly with a memory rather than the present physical connection seeming forced upon her. What flashed in her mind were the words her mother had written about Richard Simpson, the crush and the secrets. She was indeed part of a different generation, a different culture, but she was more her mother's daughter than she had realized. And when the kiss was over and Jacob backed away, Guin felt sorry for him. Guin felt as though he was her Richard Simpson.

CHAPTER 4:
ATHABASCA

i

IT WAS STILL dark when Guin and her father made the forty-five-minute flight across Great Slave Lake to Hay River on an old WWII Douglas DC-4 aircraft, but the sun had shown itself as they landed. Edmund and his pilot met them in the small airport terminal with a nod and a handshake. Edmund was short, clean-shaven, and his hair was buzzed. He didn't smile. He didn't even acknowledge Guin. The pilot had sunglasses on, hugging his fat and hairy face, lips hidden underneath a brown and gray blanket of hair.

"If you're ready," said Edmund.

"Lead the way," Eugene said.

They boarded a four-passenger Cessna Skyhawk, so it was a tight fit for her and her father in the back seats. But once they were in the air, her attention was below, where the Slave River snaked its way from Athabasca to Great Slave Lake. It was tinged green and brown in places, but mostly blue. Pockets of driftwood collected in curves, building up like beaver dams might if those beavers were the size of the shy moose lurking in the sea of dark green jack pine and black spruce dominating the land below. It all looked so flat from the air as if you could see for hundreds of miles in every direction from wherever you were standing, but when they landed, that sea of dark and light greens, that looked more like a Monet painting from the sky, obscured everything in all directions. They were surrounded here by those giants. At home, she had the expanse of the open lake to gaze out onto, her top of the world like the top of a mountain. It was almost claustrophobic here, and, for

70

the first time, she felt uneasy, her stomach quivering. It wasn't because of the trees for she felt at ease around them. The unease was due to their task. It had finally dawned on her what they were actually doing, but she was able to keep it all inside for now.

Neither Edmund nor her father had spoken much on the flight, and the pilot was silent the whole way. That didn't help her disquiet. In the taxi from the airport to the dock, she noticed a burned down building atop a red granite bluff overlooking the lake.

"What happened there?" she asked Edmund from the back seat.

"Was Fort Chipewyan Lodge . . . burned down a few years back. The locals told us a lot of things been happening around here the past couple decades." He turned around to face her, his hazel eyes more green than brown. "Annalisa thought it was an omen, that we should have stopped our research here, but—"

"Mom wouldn't hear of it."

"She was determined. Didn't let the people from the tar sands scare her off with their threats of legal action or the locals' superstitions get in her way."

He seemed more relaxed now that her mother had been brought up and that Guin hadn't broken down; instead, she spoke as if nothing had happened, as if her mother would be meeting them at the dock, even though her mind was a maelstrom.

"We were collecting data from the water and soil," Edmund said, "to see how much the tar sands had affected the region since upping production back in the 2000s. Theory is that the leaks and runoff from the tar sands have filled the Athabasca River with naphthenic acid, mercury, arsenic, lead, and other heavy metals and pollutants that have contaminated the lake here as well. The communities depend on this lake to survive. We tested around Fort Res and the Slave River to see if it moved on to your lake."

She couldn't help but want to smile when he said, "your lake," because it did feel like hers. She told it her secrets every night, trusted it to keep those secrets safe. Gazing at her reflection in its dark waters, it returned her smiles, her frowns, and it rippled away that reflection when she shed tears, for it couldn't handle seeing her cry.

"Aside from spikes in cancer and a lot of dead, deformed, or contaminated fish, over thirty people have gone missing since 2001, mostly Mikisew Cree First Nations. Fires have gotten worse.

The lodge burned down. Fort McMurray's blaze last year, which was one of the worst wildfires in Alberta's history . . . the list goes on and on. Strangest part of it all was that the Cree, the Dene, and others from the tribes actually talked to us. It's rare for them to open up to white people, but I'm glad they did."

"So, were they implying that Big Oil cronies disappeared people?" asked Eugene.

"That's the odd part. We thought the same thing, but the two didn't go together," said Edmund, shaking his head. "I mean, there's only about a thousand people here, and the ones that have gone missing weren't all necessarily activists against the tar sands."

"What did they say when you brought that up?" asked Guin.

"That's where we hit a brick wall. They'd talk all day about the runoff from the tar sands, but wouldn't budge about the missing people."

"They'll hardly talk to each other about that," said the skinny taxi driver, an older man with long black hair pulled back in a ponytail.

There were a few seconds of silence before Eugene said to the driver, "Will you?"

The driver glanced at Eugene in the rearview mirror, brown eyes meeting gray. Slightly shaking his head, he replied, "No," in a tone that wasn't disrespectful or angry, just final.

Guin understood. Even her students, whom she cared for dearly, had clear boundaries that they weren't willing to cross, no matter how much they trusted her. To them, she would always be the other, as the driver viewed all three of them now . . . as the residents had probably viewed her mother, Annalisa, and Edmund when they were taking samples and trying to understand what had happened in this tiny hamlet.

"There's a lot of desolate country up here," said Edmund. "Just because the population is small and the communities spread out doesn't give Suncor and the others the right to do what they're doing. But, if they have a hand in this, it's working because my boss is hesitant to put another team together to finish up the work regardless of the outcome of RCMP's investigation."

"Can I ask you something, Edmund?" said Guin.

"Sure."

"You know why my father and I are here. How ready are you to go back to where this happened?"

THE THING IN THE WIND

There was silence for nearly a minute, then Edmund said, "I'd be going back whether your father had asked me to or not." He turned and faced her now, the seatbelt digging into the side of his neck. "I have questions I need answered as well."

Guin nodded, then looked out the window as Edmund turned back around.

To their surprise, the driver added, "Don't count on getting answers out here. No one seems to get answers out here." His tone was ominous, but not threatening.

The taxi stopped at the dock, and Eugene paid the man. After taking the money, the driver noticed the boat that was waiting for them.

"I may stand corrected," said the driver, keeping his eyes on the boat and the two men aboard. "You might get a few answers after all."

ii

They got their backpacks out of the trunk, then approached the two men waiting for them. One was tall and skinny and the other average height and stocky wearing a toboggan. They both looked like they belonged on a fishing vessel from somewhere in the Northeastern United States like Boston or Maine, but their accents were purely Canadian.

"So," said the stocky one, "who's Eugene?"

"I am." He shook the man's hand.

"Berin van Tighem," he said. "This is my brother, Frank. Miksa's on board resting . . . you'll meet him later. So, we'll be taking the three of you across the lake to Stony Rapids, yes?"

"That's right," said Eugene. "And you've been paid."

"Indeed. Michelle's confirmed everything. We'll follow the south bank, so we're looking at two to three days of travel. A lot of bad weather along the way, all week in fact. Arranged your snowmobiles and other gear to be waiting for you in Stony Rapids, so you should be all set."

"Good."

They followed the brothers aboard a small, weathered white and blue cruising trawler with dirty windows weeping rusty tears down its side. The paint was chipped here and there, and the hull appeared to be stained green in places and orange in others at the waterline. But the deck was clean and dry, the gunwale shining in the morning sun nearly blinding Guin. She took in her first deep breath through her nose, and it made her cough. An acrid tang in the back of her throat as if from diesel and tar.

"Is that normal?" she asked anyone in earshot.

"What's that?" said Frank.

"The smell."

"No. It comes in waves. Sometimes it smells of sulphur. Sometimes of burning timber. Once we pass Greywillow Wildland it starts going away."

"It's making me sick," she said.

"Makes most of the residents at Fort Chip sick as well," Frank said. "Mainly why we stay up Camsell Portage most of the year. Tar sands, down Fort McMurray way. Done a real number on the area. Practically contaminated the whole wetlands one way or another."

"How long have you been here?" she asked, noticing the sounds of the birds' high-pitched calls coming from a cluster of birch trees by the road. She wondered if they, too, tasted the bitterness in the air.

"Used to live in Banff. Berin's lived all over Alberta . . . Calgary, Edmonton, McMurray, and even right here in Fort Chip. That's when I came up to keep him company, and then we got us a spot across the way at Camsell. Been there for a bit and can't see myself, can't see Berin, leaving. No. Not anytime soon."

"The area does have a way of keeping you here, doesn't it?" she said, wondering if she was the only one that felt such a connection with the region.

"It does. Special places up here. Takes a strong soul to handle it all. Especially the winters. So you're from these parts as well? You don't sound like it."

"Yellowknife. Three years."

"DeBeers?"

"My husband works there, yes. I teach."

"Isolated spot."

"Look who's talking," she said with a smile.

"Touché. But, you're far more remote than we are."

"I love it. Don't think I'll be leaving anytime soon either."

"Good for you. And your husband?" he asked after glancing at her ring.

"He'll come around."

THE THING IN THE WIND

With a mustard grin and a nod, Frank said, "Indeed," then bent down and loosened the hitch knot from the cleat.

The rumbling sound of the engine drowned out the birdsong, and they were off, leaving Fort Chipewyan behind without another glance. As Berin played captain, Frank directed the others to the sleeping quarters below deck. It'd be tight and uncomfortable, but it would do. Their beds were near the bow while the others were at the stern.

"Miksa's back there asleep. You'll meet him later," said Frank. "Help yourself to anything in the kitchen. We'll be fishing along the way as well." He paused a moment. "I trust you eat more than plants?" he asked Guin.

"Yes, but only if it swims."

After thanking him, they all put their packs on their beds, then joined the brothers on the main deck.

iii

The sunlight didn't last long as deep blue and gray clouds moved in from the north just as they'd reached the Athabasca River Delta and turned east to follow the southern shoreline of the lake. Clusters of willow bushes trembled in the wind, their collective sound like cold water poured into a hot skillet. Behind their clusters, boggy wetlands devoid of human inhabitance stretched for miles as far as they could see. In a month or two, it would all be covered in a thick blanket of snow and ice.

Even though the wind dropped the temperature just below freezing, Guin stayed up top on the main deck watching the dancing willows, watching the migrating birds disappear in the tall grass to rest, and tried to come up with something to say to her father, who stood a few feet from her and seemed to be enjoying Nature just as much as she had been since getting on the boat. To her relief, he spoke first, but neither of them broke their gaze from the willows, as if they'd seen them for the first time and would never see them again once they'd moved on from the delta.

"Your mother, if she is indeed dead, died doing what she loved."

"I know, Dad."

"I think her work was the only thing that kept us together, you know."

"Yours, too. Both of you put work first." In her periphery, she saw that he was looking at her, but didn't take her eyes off the endless willows swaying in the light breeze.

"I'm sorry."

"Nothing to be sorry about. Your jobs gave you both fulfillment, made you happy."

"But—"

"No buts . . . I never felt unloved, but I didn't inherit that trait from either of you. This," she said, pointing to a collection of boulders spattered with light green lichen and surrounded by thick moss, "is my passion." She looked at him. "I want to be rooted. Want to have one place that I call home. And a place that doesn't change too much."

"I know what Jefferson meant to you."

Guin could feel a twinge of adrenaline in her chest, knowing that the conversation was about to get difficult.

"Your mom knew. That was really our first argument."

Her stomach tightened. She had stopped reading her mother's journals in Jefferson because she thought that she'd been experiencing it all firsthand, but that wasn't true. She'd never read about them arguing. It ignited a fire in her instantly, and she wanted to read them all. Wanted to know it all from her mother's perspective, as she'd been accustomed to for so much of her mother's history.

"She wanted me to retire." He smiled, but moisture had built up in his eyes. A kiss of wind helped him hold back a tear. "Said she wanted to see you pick apples from your own orchard."

There was no knot in her throat to let her know that tears were coming, no other warning, just a few hints of laughter, the kind that mixed both happiness and sadness, and the tears fell copiously.

Guin's father embraced her as he said, "But we couldn't stay. The company your mother worked for, Blackwood, has offices all over North America, and they do good work. When Denver came up for me, they wanted her there immediately, wanted her to work on the Rocky Flats project." He looked at her now. "But *you* always came first."

"I know, Dad." She knew it was true. They never took her somewhere that she felt unsafe, somewhere that she didn't get a good education or other opportunities, or put her in harm's way. Always seemed to kill two birds with one stone . . .

THE THING IN THE WIND

"I mean it, Guin." He stepped back, watching his daughter wipe off her glasses and dry her eyes with the sleeves of her wool jacket. "I know the moving was hard, but you always seemed to adjust even more quickly than we did."

"I did." She had gotten control of her emotions. "I don't have any regrets."

"Promise? All that time alone didn't bother you?"

"Promise," she said quickly. And she meant it. It made her think of Jacob. Was she keeping him in Yellowknife selfishly? Was she putting herself first, even though she knew that he absolutely hated everything about the north? According to her father, her parents were seemingly a healthy mix of selfish and selfless, but *she* was all about herself. She was the only one benefiting by staying in Yellowknife. Each day that they stayed there, she could see another tiny sliver of Jacob get sliced away. How would she do on her own? If she divorced Jacob and let him leave the frigid north, would they both be happier? Her salary at Aurora College could certainly cover the house payment, so that wasn't an issue. Did she really love him or was he just safe? Someone that she could control and do with as she pleased, unlike Anton who would have been like her father, moving without a real choice in the matter. And did she really want that if it was true? Maybe not, she thought, turning her gaze back to the clusters of willows, back to the expanse of a world uninhabited by humans. A wild and desolate place. Maybe she just wanted to be alone, at the top of the world, in a place where few people crossed her path, a place where she could be one with Nature, one with the cosmos. One where it was only her, if that's how she wanted it to be. There was only one thing nagging her: the journals. So, while they were being honest with each other, she let it out: "Do you have all of Mom's journals?"

"I do. Back in Anchorage."

"I want them," she said. "All of them."

"I'll mail them to you when I get back."

"Did she keep writing? In San Antonio and Anchorage?"

He finally smiled. "She did. Every night."

Hesitating for a moment, she said, "Did she—"

"She did," he said, smile still on his face. "At least she suspected."

Guin nodded as the wind picked up again, throwing her hair to the side violently as it did with the willows and birch and jack pine trees farther in on the mainland. So her mother had known. Guin only hoped that her mother hadn't withheld any thoughts or, well, anything from the journals since finding out that her daughter had been reading them. It would make it all a lie. Make it so that she didn't feel like she really knew her mother at all. Well, at least completely.

"I'm glad," Guin said.

"So was she."

The early journals that Guin had read introduced her to her grandparents, had given her a firsthand look at what it meant to be strong, independent, and go after what you want. The successes and failures . . . how her grandmother, Penny, had gotten a glimpse of that independence, then gave in to the pressures of society and religion. Her mother, the success, breaking out and making her own path. Both of them writers who wrote for themselves and their daughters. And that's where the line would be broken, Guin knew. Her journals didn't have a little one that could go and find them and read them. She had made that clear to Jacob very early on in their relationship. She had no siblings, so there'd be no nieces or nephews to tell the stories to or to get to know. No. When she died, it'd be the end of the line, the trilogy complete, and she was okay with that, even though she knew that her position was unique. And deep down, she knew that Jacob didn't agree with her position, but was willing to make the sacrifice. So, Guin wrote in her journals for her and her alone. She was okay with that, too.

The sleet didn't give much warning, as it seemed to pour out of the dark clouds suddenly. Had Edmund or the brothers looked their way at that moment, they wouldn't have known either had been crying because they were soaked in less than a minute. They found refuge in the wheelhouse with Berin, Edmund, and Frank.

"I'm surprised it's still raining," said Berin, "this late in the year."

"By the sound, it's a mix," said Frank.

Berin started talking about the weather patterns, about how it'd been warmer for longer that October, and then shifted to how many people had gone missing each year, that the number kept increasing and how the authorities kept ignoring it.

"They don't care what happens up here," said Berin. "Ghost towns from port to port. Uranium City, Gunnar, Fond du Lac, they all used to have hundreds, some thousands back when the mines were in operation. Now, ghost towns. Hollowed-out frames of what they used to be. Sure, you have a few that hold on, that claim they love the desolation and the outdoors, that they love the peace and quiet, but what are they holding on to out here? There's nothing left. What is left is dying from the tar sands. Why do they stay?"

Guin felt herself going back to the classroom where she taught about similar issues when she blurted out, "Why are *you* still here?"

Berin fell silent immediately, shifting his gaze from the water to Guin. His answer did not need to be spoken, for his eyes told it all, but he said it anyway: "Unfinished business."

She did not respond, just nodded once. She didn't need the specifics to know that something weighed on him the same way something weighed on her father. But with her father, she knew and needed to know. With Berin, it was his burden, and she had nothing to do with it.

By the door was a dark green slicker. Guin put it on, exited the wheelhouse, and went back to her spot on the main deck, watching the treetops sway, the willow clusters rustle and bend, and felt the cold wind caress her face as it slid up from the dark water of Lake Athabasca.

iv

The sleet ceased about an hour after nightfall, but the wind kept howling, pushing the remaining clouds away from them. Guin was not tired, so she sat on deck and listened to the sounds emerging from the black forest ashore while gazing up at the night sky. In Jefferson, the stars had not been easy to see. Sure, Polaris was obvious, but the dimmer stars were not visible. Denver was darker at night back then, let her see a few more. And Yellowknife was a whole new world, as she saw thousands more burning up there in the cold darkness on cloudless nights like this, but some of those were hidden by the polar lights. Here, anchored somewhere on Lake Athabasca where there were no lights burning on the ground, she saw millions up there, and it made her wonder how many of those stars had died already but whose lights had not been completely extinguished. Wasn't that what the astronomers had said, that many of the stars you see in the night sky are actually dead, but the way light works, the way it moves through space shows us history, not real-time life in the cosmos? It was a frightening thought, that what she saw and perceived to be alive was actually dead, that the night sky was history, and she'd never be able to catch up. Was it like that on Earth, too? Were psychics just scientists who understood and could see what the masses could not? If so, what would they see if they looked at her? Someone who had died long ago, but who others could still see because she had not been extinguished yet? Or maybe she was still alive and well, but what about her father? Had he died? Was she just seeing him before he became a ghost? A shade? And what would that mean for her mother? How long ago had she really died? A few months? Years? This kind of thinking upset her. She wasn't an astrophysicist, wasn't a psychic. She was flesh and blood in a desolate part of the world, trying to understand her place in it all, but she couldn't. Back in Jefferson, she could. Back in Jefferson, she was young and innocent. Wanted an orchard. That was all. Now, she was married. Her mother was probably dead. She was an investigator with no training.

Whistling wind snaking its way through the boreal forest snagged her attention. For the first time in days, she felt hungry, but she didn't crave food. Her stomach just wanted . . . something. When she stood, a gust almost knocked her back down, but she grabbed the gunwale for balance. It was invigorating, that wind, and she wanted to be ashore running through the trees as fast as she could with the wind at her back. And she smiled at that thought, closed her eyes and imagined the rocking deck was the forest floor, her feet running so fast that they barely made contact. Like flying. Her smile widened as images of soaring just above the tree line, the prickly pine treetops tickling the bottoms of her feet, stole her imagination. Then, it stopped abruptly, and she opened her eyes, seeing only the foggy lenses of her glasses. Her heart jackhammered the back of her chest, deep gasps of air icing her lungs. Normally, this would hurt, but tonight it was soothing. She felt dizzy as if drugged, then decided it was best to make her way below with the others, so she wiped her glasses again and did just that.

For the first time, she felt out of place—the woman who had strolled into the packed men's room. They all got quiet and turned their gazes toward her.

It was awkward for only a moment, then she said, "I guess I need a beer to join this party."

THE THING IN THE WIND

Like snapping out of hypnosis, it did the trick, and Frank reached for a Molson.

"Just kidding. I'm good. Is the other guy sick or something?" she asked, her head still spinning.

"Miksa," said Berin. "He sleeps a lot. And he's shy." He took a gulp of Molson from his bottle. "I wouldn't be surprised if you all don't meet him."

"Why?" she asked slowly.

An uncomfortable silence, then Berin repeated, "He's shy."

She didn't push it any further. The experience on deck, the dizziness and confusion, it made her bid the others a good night and then lay down. She kept the door open, but the room stayed quite dark. Edmund had loosened up and finally started talking more after a beer. They'd taken samples every thirty kilometers. The people they came across were kind. Once they were at camp along the river between Stony Rapids and Black Lake, something happened in the middle of the night. Edmund left his tent to pee.

"The fire had burned down to glowing embers, just enough light to see the tents. Shirley and Annalisa's tent was unzipped. I called out and got no answer, then looked in with a flashlight. Nothing. It'd been dry, so there were no footprints to follow. They weren't by the river. They didn't respond to my calls. I didn't know what to do except radio for help. Help came. About an hour after sunrise, we found Shirley's coat in a clearing about a kilometer and a half into the woods. Never found a trace of Annalisa."

Guin realized that he refrained from mentioning when they'd found the rest of her mother's things . . . and the bones that her father had mentioned.

"Is that why you're going back?" asked Berin.

"I don't know why I'm going back. It goes against my better judgment."

"Gut feeling?" asked Frank.

"It's not that," Edmund continued. "My gut told me to stay home. Logic told me to stay home. But, something else, some strange pull. And I'm not a spiritual person, so it's not that either. But, something I can't describe or recognize, but it's hidden in there," he pointed to his chest, "or there," he pointed to his head, "and I just don't know how to shut it up or ignore it, so here I am, away from civilization and home again, heading back into the wilderness."

81

"Unfinished business," said Eugene.

"Maybe," said Edmund. "But if it is, I don't feel like it's mine."

Guin heard two short spurts of air in succession.

"I can understand that," said Berin, "enough to know we both need another drink."

"Cheers to that," said Edmund.

Someone started talking again, but the sound was muffled in Guin's ears as her heavy eyelids closed. She listened to the creeping wind, the lapping lake water hugging the hull, and cacophony of nocturnal wildlife. It only lasted a few minutes before Guin fell asleep on the uncomfortable foam mattress.

V

The word came from a far-off place where wind is born. It woke the boy. Moonlight glowed through his lone window as shadows of gale-blown hemlock and juniper danced on the floor like deranged demons clawing their way past the veil on a Samhain night. Vision blurry with sleep dust, he glanced at indistinct shapes until locking on to the black sliver between the jamb and closet door—

Guin knew that it was the dream again, the one she'd been having for over a week, but it was lucid this time. It was the same as she'd read in her mother's journal. There was a difference this time. It wasn't from the boy's perspective as it had been, and it wasn't like watching it on a television as her mother had described it. This dream made her presence there, invisible, in that room with him.

Max was covered in sweat and peering toward the closet, but Guin didn't feel his fear as she had before. No, she tried to analyze it all this time: the fear of something lurking in the closet, the fascination of watching his grotesque reflection in the warped windowpane, the stuffed moose head staring down at him in the firelight. None of it seemed to matter except . . . yes, the voice that called for him out there in the cold. "*Max*," it coaxed. The sound was uncanny, something that couldn't have come from a human. The kind of sound the wind might make when trying to mimic a person's voice. How had she not picked up on that sooner? And what about her mother? None of the entries mentioned anything about the sound other than its siren-song seductiveness, its power to make you investigate its source.

THE THING IN THE WIND

She followed Max as he zigzagged through the forest, looking left and right to see what else she may have missed. Nothing. Darkness. She looked up at the bright full moon, at the stars that were visible beyond the shivering treetops, searching for any missing piece. And she stopped, the sound of Max's feet mashing down the fresh snow becoming distant, but she knew where he was going. It wasn't her gut, but a tingling in her spine that told her to stop and stare up at those stars. It happened in a split second—the stars of Eridanus, to Pegasus, to the watchful eyes of Draco, they all shifted slightly as if a filter had been placed over Guin's eyes. As quickly as the filter had been placed, it had been taken away, and the stars were normal again. It filled her with momentary awe and wonder.

"Max!" She heard from the darkness, followed by piercing and screeching wind.

Guin ran, following Max's footprints in the snow.

"Max!" She heard again, this time much louder.

By the time she reached the glade, Max had already been taken. She searched for remnants of his tracks, most of which had been filled in with fresh snow. The deepest prints were surrounded with broken tree limbs. Instinctively, Guin looked up and east, noticed damage to the nearest tree, and shuddered when the giant red eye Betelgeuse shifted for only a split second.

Then she woke up.

Vİ

The thump came from above. No, it wasn't a thump. More like a splat, the way a slushy snowball might sound when it crashes onto pavement. Footsteps outside the room. They were going up on deck.

Guin slipped out of bed, went up the narrow staircase, and stopped at the top when she heard the muffled sound of men's voices. She recognized Frank's deep voice, along with Berin's.

". . . trouble, brother," said Frank.

"Look, Frank, you didn't have to come along if you didn't want to. We're getting good money to be chauffeurs," said Berin.

"You haven't been past the dunes in ages, and I can't blame you. It's been even longer since Stony Rapids," said Frank.

"Enough! I know you're concerned with the area. I know the stories, too. For God's sake, we're part of those stories."

83

Guin's stomach churned at these words. She was familiar with some of the history of the place, but that had all been stories from long ago, nothing so recent as to involve these two. It worried her, making her forget about the sound she'd heard. Is that what the taxi driver had meant? That these two white men had some arcane knowledge about the place that the First Nations people would never reveal? Guin kept herself hidden.

"What do you mean we're part of the stories?" asked Frank.

"Julia," said Berin. "That was the last place anyone saw her."

"I know."

"But what you don't know is that I found something when I walked from Stony Rapids to Black Lake."

There was a long pause.

"It was her wedding ring."

Guin's throat tightened. Maybe *they* knew something about her mother. Maybe it wasn't a coincidence that they were the chauffeurs. As much as she wanted to turn the corner and demand answers to the questions swirling in her mind—What happened in this area? Did you know my mother? Do you know anything about her disappearance? What the fuck is really going on here?—she knew that the smart decision was to stay put and soak up the rest of their conversation. Maybe they'd answer the questions without her asking.

"Why didn't you tell me?" asked Frank.

"I didn't tell anyone. It's not something that needs to be told."

"And you're sure it's hers?"

"Yes, it has a small engraving on the inside that confirmed it." Berin paused again. "This man, he's here for a reason. And I'm going with him."

"So, this is why you brought all that *stuff* with us?"

"Yes, Frank." Berin took in a deep breath, then exhaled loudly. "You have no idea how much I miss her. How hard it is to fall asleep in a lonely bed. Only to get to sleep and dream that she's beside you"—his voice began to crack—"to wake up, and suddenly have her taken away from you all over again." His words were a whisper by the time he finished.

"I'm sorry, Berin." There was another pause before Frank said, "I'll go with you. Miksa can stay on board."

So that's what it was. He didn't know anything. The same thing had happened to him. He was just like her . . . looking for answers. Guin heard the cabin door shut.

THE THING IN THE WIND

Frank was standing outside, shaking his head. He didn't see her immediately, not until Guin turned the corner. It was the flickering light on Frank's face that drew her out. When she got on deck, she saw the fires along the shoreline.

"What's going on, Frank?"

Frank pointed to the back of the boat. There was a glistening mound of something there about the size of a basketball. "That was thrown on deck."

The firelight reflected in the expanding, dark pool forming from the mound.

"What is it?" asked Guin, holding her nose. "It smells awful."

"It's a warning," said Frank. "These parts are considered cursed lands by the Cree."

"Cursed?" she said, as her father and Edmund emerged from below deck. "What—"

"Like Berin said, they're very superstitious in these parts," said Frank, approaching and then kneeling down next to the mutilation. "It's caribou. Rotten caribou."

"I don't understand," said Guin. "If the lands are cursed, then why are they still living here?"

"To keep us out," said Berin.

Guin could feel her mother's frustration boiling up inside her; she never allowed elements of the supernatural to cloud her path or judgment, and Guin felt similarly. She wouldn't stay silent about it either.

"Can you please be more specific? How are these cursed lands and why do they want to keep us out? It doesn't make sense."

"And why didn't they try to keep us out before?" asked Edmund.

Berin, with fire reflecting in his eyes, replied, "You were all trying to help, trying to make sure the water wasn't contaminated. I can only assume that they found that to be a noble cause designed to keep the area protected. And, because of that, you wouldn't have any trouble, that the curse wouldn't apply to you."

"You cannot expect us to believe that they were victims of a curse," Guin said. "So—"

"I don't expect you to believe anything," said Berin. "And I don't care what you believe. It's not my place to try and convince you of anything. You wanted to know what all this meant, and I told you." Berin pointed to the fires. "The people out there believe

85

there's a curse. They stay on the periphery. They warn people . . . in their own way."

"Have you heard of a wendigo?" asked Frank.

The word made her shudder, but it also gave her clarity. Why hadn't she put it together before? The dream! The boy, Max, he'd been summoned from that cabin by a wendigo. And the great moose . . . some incarnation? Guin tried to swallow at the next revelation, but her throat was too dry. The new version of the dream that she'd just been stirred from a few minutes ago. It was too hideous to imagine, too frightening to dwell upon. The shimmer in the stars . . .

Guin only nodded slowly because she was unable to speak.

"Good. Because out here, it's not just considered lore," said Frank, taking a step toward Guin. "Are you okay?"

This question made everyone turn their attention on her.

"Guin?" her father said. "What is it?"

"Nothing," she said. "What were you saying, Frank?"

"Are you sure?" asked Frank.

"I said it's nothing."

Her tone said a lot more that all of them understood. Whatever they thought was wrong with her was none of their business and they needed to leave it alone.

"There's recent talk of a wendigo in this region," said Frank.

"And they call that a curse," said Berin. "I've not heard of any member of any of the tribes ever giving the full details about wendigos."

The reflecting fire in Berin's eyes made Guin quiver again, as if she were young and sitting around a campfire, listening to the old wise man begin a tale of terror.

"The chief down in Black Lake gave me a few details about them, and a friend in Camsell helped give me insight into what I was dealing with as well, but the most troubling bit that he finished with continues to haunt me." Berin spoke slowly, deliberately. "He said that the anthropologists, the writers, and anyone else not part of the tribes know less than one percent about wendigos, and of that knowledge, half was false." He paused, shifting his gaze to the fires near the shoreline. "That any white man seeking the creature would have to hunt it blindly."

"They didn't give you more insight?" asked Guin.

Berin met Guin's eyes and shook his head.

THE THING IN THE WIND

"I've never heard of fires on the shoreline or rotten caribou being warning signs," Guin said.

"Like I said, outsiders know very little," Berin replied.

"Aside from them," Guin said, pointing to the shoreline, "what does this have to do with us?"

Berin reached into his pocket and retrieved his wallet. Inside, he slipped out a photo and handed it to Guin. "That's my wife, Julia."

Guin studied it for a moment, then handed the photo to her father.

"A few years ago, we'd just moved into a house back there in Fort Chip. She'd just started a new job. Her first assignment was a trip to Fir Island, a short boat ride from the Black Lake settlement. I hugged and kissed her goodbye. She made it to Stony Rapids, met her driver, and was never seen again."

"Berin . . . " said Guin, "I-I—"

"Please, no words." He paused. "But, when we get to Stony Rapids, there's a slight change of plans."

"How exactly are the plans changing?" asked Eugene.

Guin noticed that her father felt threatened by these words based on his tone. Lowering the photo, he looked to be readying himself for whatever might come next.

"I'm coming with you."

As quickly as Guin noticed her father's shift in demeanor, she then saw it wither. He understood now.

Unfinished business, Eugene mouthed.

"I have to face whatever's out there, whatever answers I can find. It's the only thing I have left to do that has any level of meaning. And when Julia disappeared"—his chin began to quiver slightly—"the locals pointed to it being a wendigo. I've stayed here, waiting. Inquiring. Searching. Seeking any answer I can, but I'm left with nothing." The words came out slowly, deliberately. "I'm not leaving this time without those answers. I don't care if I come back or not."

Guin didn't know what to say, but her father didn't hesitate to jump in: "You're certainly welcome to come along, Berin. We'd be glad to have you."

Berin nodded. As his chin settled, he said, "The tribes won't cause us any further trouble. They've done their part." He turned away from them and toward the rotten mass of caribou. "You should both get some sleep, and I'll get this cleaned up."

Guin wasn't going to bring it up now, but she wondered why Berin hadn't mentioned the wedding ring. If he had found something there, shouldn't he have told them? After all, it would fit the pattern of something being left behind. Julia's ring. Her mother's scarf. Guin figured that the man had his reasons, so she let it go but didn't forget.

They went to the room, but they did not sleep yet. How could they?

"Dad—"

"It's going to be okay." He shook his head. "You have to understand, Guin, I just need answers, and no one has them. This is the only place I can search for them my way. If I come up short, then I'll have to leave it, but at least I'll know that I tried." Eugene dropped to his bed as if both knees had given out. "I can live with that, I think." He put his right hand to his forehead and began rubbing as if trying to massage away a headache. "If I come up empty, I *hope* I can live with it and not be in the same state Berin's in."

"Please try and get some rest now, Dad."

She watched as he lay back and closed his eyes. Once Guin heard snoring, she slid the thick blanket off her and crept out of the room and back up on deck. The freezing air went straight to her bones after being so warm and snug below, but she didn't let that deter her from staring at the dying fires along the shoreline. She didn't see any people, just the flames licking the cold air. Why was she here? Sure, for her father, but what did it all mean to her?

When she thought this, the next thought was of Jacob. The man, her husband, was miserable up here. Her mother had probably died, even if the circumstances were unknown at this point. And Guin wasn't going to immediately give in to a supernatural cause. Her father was here, clearly not in a healthy mental state. So, how and why did she feel so good here? It caused a few slivers of guilt to creep into her, the kind that sits and festers in your gut. Why did she feel this guilt? Why couldn't she be strong like her mother had been? When she had been in Tennessee, her entire plan revolved around escaping. The woman left her parents, boyfriend, everything without shedding a tear. There was no hesitation to leave, no remorse, and no looking back. Once Shirley had crossed the Tennessee state line, she'd never crossed it again.

It all made her think of Jacob. There was that deep, hidden feeling within her, slightly deeper than the cold air that had reached her bones, that told her that if she were to stay in the north, to stay in Yellowknife for good, Jacob would not be with her. He didn't have the desire, the love for the place that she did. He was going crazy, but her crazy was being cured. Wouldn't it be the honest thing to do to begin divorce proceedings when she returned? Or would it just be selfish? She thought about that for a few moments. Some of the fires burned down to glowing embers, shining bright when the breeze went by and sending with it the calming aroma of campfire. No. It had to be done. Yes, she loved him, and this was how she would show him that love, by setting him free and divorcing him. By not dragging it all out to the point when he would feel too old to begin a new relationship.

She heard a knock behind her, too light to make her startle, and, before she could react, felt something soft on the back of her neck and shoulders.

"Thought you'd be asleep."

She recognized the voice. It was Frank. Before she responded, she pulled up the blanket he had brought her, wrapped it around her body, then turned around. And when she realized the difference, she let out a "Hmmph."

"What is it?" Frank said.

It was the difference in response, and it hit her immediately. Had it been Jacob, she would have shunned him, mostly ignored him the way she had a few days ago on the dock. But with Frank, she accepted. She turned around and acknowledged him, but she would not tell him that.

"Not as easy as I thought it'd be," she said with a smirk.

"Yeah," he responded, letting out a nervous laugh. "That makes two of us."

"What's your reason?"

"I've always been a light sleeper," he said. "And, my brother. He's not in a good place."

"What do you mean?" She knew that she was prying, but another part of her knew that Frank's brother was their ride, so any problems with him immediately concerned her.

"Just dealing with some old demons." He crossed his arms. "It looks like this trip will be important to all of us."

"Thanks for not really answering the question." She meant this as a joke, but she immediately realized that Frank didn't see it that way.

"Sorry. It's just something I can't talk about right now, okay?"

"I was just joking, Frank."

"Oh." He let himself smile and ease the momentary tension. "He brought up Julia and gave the gist, but there's more to it all than just a disappearance." He shook his head. "Nothing that pertains to what we're doing out here."

Guin nodded and said "Okay" before turning back around.

"I'm gonna grab a beer. You want one?"

As he asked this, Guin had turned her gaze to the water, the boat's light emanating just enough for her to see her reflection. While it was similar to Great Slave Lake, it was not her lake, and a terrible pang in her gut swirled . . . not painful, more like the feeling of missing someone. "I do," she said, then swallowed the knot that had crept into her throat.

While Frank was gone, Guin turned off the boat light. The gust came when she was back at her post, a gust unlike the others had been. This one carried with it a pungent odor that she couldn't place. Hadn't Frank mentioned that the wind sometimes carried the stink of sulphur or timber? This was far from that . . . something wild like caribou or moose fur crossed with disturbed bogland with the sharp bitterness of ammonia. And then it dawned on her that it smelled of ozone, that was the word. It made her shiver and nearly gag for the few seconds it lingered, and then it was gone. Tongues of flames not yet transformed to embers licked the darkness violently, bending to the will of the wind that carried the odor across the shoreline.

No, this was certainly not her lake. Her lake would never make her feel this kind of unease. Would never make her feel like an interloper. It was a deeper disquiet than the tribes could have made her feel; this ran to the very core of her soul.

The hiss of escaping air broke her concentration.

"Beer," said Frank.

"I definitely need this," she said while turning around and taking the frigid bottle of Molson. She drank half the bottle in her first gulp. What was it about beer being cold that always seemed right? It didn't matter if the temperature was ninety or nine degrees, beer needed to be cold.

"Cheers," said Frank.

"Oops. Sorry." Her bottle met his, and then she took a smaller gulp this time.

"It's no problem," he said with a smile, then took a drink of his own.

"Did you catch that odor a minute ago? It was very different than before."

"I didn't."

She let it go for now. If it happened again, she thought, then she'd make a bigger deal of it. "Do you have anyone, Frank? Other than Berin?"

"No," he said. "A few girlfriends a long time ago back in Banff, but nothing came of 'em."

Guin nodded.

"Since coming up this way, I've had a different perspective. A different purpose." He took another drink. "Kinda had to do that if I was to make it up here."

"What do you mean?"

"To survive up here. Small population. White skin's not the most popular. Anyway, I'm sure I'll break away sometime, head back south and start up a new chapter."

"I'm tired of starting new chapters," Guin said, then paused for a few seconds. "You're a good brother to Berin. A kind soul."

Frank smiled, then looked down at his feet. "I appreciate you saying that." After taking another drink, Frank said, "I think I'll head down now. You all right?"

"Yeah. Just gonna stay up here a little while longer." So, he wasn't going to bring up the ring either. Maybe that was what he'd meant by old demons. After all, he'd just found out about the ring and Berin's plans a few hours ago and possibly hadn't processed it all. She could understand that, but it still irked her that this little detail was being concealed when it could prove to have much more significance.

vii

Guin finished her beer and made her way to bed not long after Frank had. An icy gale rocked the boat as she reached out to open the door to her and her father's quarters. Grabbing the rail to balance herself, she hesitated while opening the door, then a shiver crawled along her spine the same way it had when she'd smelled the odd odor on deck, but there was something more this time. That static feeling at the base of your skull when you know that you're being watched. Guin wanted to turn, but her body was stiff. She just stood there, right hand gripping the rail so tightly it ached.

Why am I afraid?

Images of the fires on shore, the splattering sound of caribou flesh, the stink of sulphur and ozone. The dull ache in her hand sharpened and gave her clarity. As she started turning around, her fear mounted the way a child's does when contemplating which monsters are lurking under the bed. But, unlike that silly child, Guin's senses were right. There was someone watching her. A face stared from a partially opened door across the room. Her mouth opened to scream, but, as if she'd had the wind knocked out of her, no sound emerged. It wasn't that there was actually someone there that startled her. It wasn't the bald head, the emaciated face, or the wild and fiery hellish eyes of the person either. It was the familiarity. She knew that face. She'd seen it before many times, but she'd seen it healthier and younger. Guin took in a deep breath, her body back in her control now.

"Max?"

VIII

They woke to heavy snowfall. Frank and Berin had caught a lake trout and arctic grayling before bringing the anchor up, getting the motor rumbling to life, and getting the trawler heading east again, crossing into Saskatchewan just after eight o'clock that morning.

Guin was alone in the room, lying in bed replaying the incident in her mind. The face that had been watching her ducked back into its room when she finally spoke, and she remained standing there, staring at the closed door for what had felt like an hour.

Was it possible that the boy from her recurring dream was on this boat? If so, it meant that she'd have to adjust her perception of the world. And what about her mother's recurring dream? He'd have to be connected to it as well. Not wanting this to continue stirring around in her mind, Guin got up and knocked on his door. When there was no answer, she tried the handle, but the door was locked. Rather than pounding on the door or calling for whoever was inside to answer, she climbed up on deck.

"Frank," she called.

He was staring toward the shore, at least she thought the shore was in that direction. The dense snow obscured their line of sight in all directions.

"Good morning," he said.

She approached him, ignoring his pleasantry. "I want to meet the person below deck."

"Miksa, sure." He swallowed hard. "Is everything okay?"

Guin nodded, biting her bottom lip. "Yeah."

She could tell that he didn't believe her, but he didn't push it. Instead, he just led her below, knocked on Miksa's door, and called for him to answer. A few seconds later, she heard a click, then watched the door open slowly.

Guin held her breath, anticipating the face of the victim in her nightmare, that aged and emaciated face of the young boy, Max, who had been coaxed out of a warm cabin and drawn to a clearing where the great moose awaited him. Where it transformed into some invisible creature and flung him high into the icy night sky. Her heart rate doubled as his hand emerged from the dark room and into the light. And it almost doubled again when she heard the recluse's voice, this hollow and distant sound that seemed somewhat muffled by a layer of dust.

"Yeah, Frank," Miksa said, opening the door all the way now so that the light hit his face.

Guin's mouth fell open again as it had the previous night, but not for the same reason. This man had hair. His skin had deep wrinkles and wear like those who live in harsh conditions . . . a lot of sun, a lot of wind. And his eyes, they were normal hazel eyes, not the wild yellowish tint she'd thought she'd seen just a few hours ago.

"Wanted you to meet one of our guests. Guin."

Guin realized that her mouth was open and quickly closed it.

Miksa's gaze met hers, and he said, "Yes." He smiled an almost toothless smile, save his K-9s up top and a few imperfect incisors on the bottom. "Didn't mean to cause you a scare last night."

"Oh—"

"What happened last night?" asked Frank.

"I was going to get a drink, and I frightened her. I figured it best to just get back in my room. Not cause any further mess."

"I'm sorry about that," Guin said. And she was, but this all confused her. The person she'd seen last night was not this man. Surely a beer wouldn't have caused her to make that big of a gaff. "I was just really tired and jumpy last night."

"No harm," said Miksa. "I better get back to my work."

With that, he retreated into his dark quarters and closed the door.

"Are you sure you're okay?" asked Frank.

"Yeah, I am now," she lied. She could tell that Frank was about to ask more questions, so she started for the stairs and asked, "Will this weather slow us down?"

Frank followed, saying, "No, but we can expect a lot more from where this is coming from, so we better get used to it."

On deck, Edmund and her father were chatting with Berin in the wheelhouse, each with a paper plate full of breakfast in one hand and a hot cup of coffee nearby.

Frank hadn't followed her up, but he called, "Do you want me to warm your breakfast and bring it up?"

She hadn't been thinking about food, but the sight of the others eating and now Frank bringing it up made her nearly ravenous. Her stomach felt suddenly empty and in need of sustenance.

"Absolutely! As long as you don't mind."

"Don't mind a bit."

Guin joined the others inside, catching the end of Berin describing Banff. The wheelhouse had that fishy smell found on most boats, but it was toned down by the scent of toasted cinnamon bread, hash browns, coffee, and the heavy aroma of bacon.

"And you'll never go back?" asked Edmund.

"Just my ashes, I suppose," said Berin.

Frank was quick to bring her breakfast and coffee, and she was thankful that he remembered not to add the bacon.

"We caught some fish earlier. Be our dinner," Frank said.

"If this clears up enough," Berin chimed in, "you might get a glimpse of the sand dunes if they're not fully covered by the snow. It's an interesting phenomenon in this area . . . like a small desert surrounded by a glacier-scarred landscape and endless forest."

Guin noticed Frank's concerned look, the way he gazed down, furrowed his brow, and seemed to grind his teeth a bit. It made her wonder whether there was something else they hadn't told them about this region.

THE THING IN THE WIND

ix

At dinner, the fish, mashed potatoes, corn, and bread were abundant enough to feed double, but they ate it all, not pausing to say much to each other. In fact, the only words spoken were from Berin to Frank, making sure he'd given Miksa a plate, which he had. After they'd discarded the paper plates and first round of beers, there was actual conversation. Guin stayed this time, but no one seemed to mention their situation. Instead, the discussion was about politics, world news, and the weather. Was it because she was there, the only woman, and they weren't comfortable doing so? Or had they just exhausted the subject, and the only thing left to do was wait and move forward once they'd arrived at Stony Rapids?

Tired of the group after half an hour, Guin took another beer and climbed up to the deck and into the wheelhouse. It was still snowing, but the weary wind didn't gust like it had earlier. It was only a minute later that Frank joined her.

"I get bored with those topics quickly, too. Mind if I join ya?"

She shook her head.

"If you don't mind my asking, what happened between you and Miksa? You seemed upset."

"He just scared me last night, that's all." She downed a gulp of beer.

"He is a bit of an odd bird, but he's a good person."

"What's his story?"

Frank paused a moment, turning his gaze outside toward the falling snow. "Lived with his father in a cabin north of Fond du Lac near McKenzie Lake. When the old man died, it was middle of winter. Miksa was only about eight. No means of communication and the snowmobile keys were kept in a safe. Well, he ran out of food and tried to walk back to the village. Got lost, but he didn't stop. He didn't know how long he'd been out in the elements, but when he reached Fond du Lac, his feet were swollen and black with frostbite, along with a few fingers."

"Oh my god! The poor thing . . ."

"He's lucky to have survived. So, when we said that he's shy, that's part of the reason. Lost both feet and three fingers. Met him when we moved to Camsell Portage. He was there, living in a small shack of a house. Berin would go to his place every few days, and they'd just talk. Endless talking."

"What'd they talk about?"

"I don't know. I was never invited, and Berin never discussed it." He downed a quarter of the bottle. "I suppose they talked about the stuff those who have experienced extreme trauma talk about, and I can't tell you what that is because I don't know."

"And Miksa never spoke to you about it?"

"Miksa hasn't spoken much more than pleasantries and shallow topics to me. We're friendly, but the real connection is between him and Berin." He took a long gulp of beer before adding, "And I'm okay with that."

Guin understood more now. Those times she'd be out on the dock, alone, or writing in her journal, alone, Jacob's presence wasn't welcome. She wanted that solitude. And when she'd pack up the tent and provisions and go out into the forest surrounding Yellowknife, it was a struggle to work up the courage to pack it all back up and go home. It was the kind of conversation she regretted never having had with her mother, Shirley. While there was plenty in her mother's journals about that special place behind the house back in Tennessee, that place that was now a highway, she still wanted to hear her mother talk about it. To ask her mother questions about what might not have made it onto those sacred pages. And to know if the energy, desire, and comfort she felt while standing on the dock over Great Slave Lake or hidden away in the jack pine and spruce and moss was indeed the same, and if her mother still felt that pull. Of course! Shirley indeed felt that pull or else she wouldn't have continued doing field work. She wouldn't have constantly fled the overpopulated cities, the loud machinery, and the ever-present hum of technology and the waves it emitted, in order to get out into the wilderness under the guise of environmental work. To talk to her mother and learn if that pull was what drove all of her actions. To hopefully gain some understanding about herself and why she continued to do the same thing, only Guin's couldn't be disguised as work. Guin's couldn't be explained easily to a wonderful husband that would never understand and wanted civilization and materialism and society's numbness. A husband, she knew, she'd have to let go if only he'd let the knot be undone.

"Why are you okay being up here, besides being the good

brother? I mean, the country is beautiful and there aren't many people, but, from what I've heard, Banff is equally if not more beautiful and there aren't *that* many people, except during tourist season."

"That's true," he said. "But, I lived my whole life there in Banff. I had an understanding of the city over in Calgary, but it was too big for me." He took another drink, then sucked in a deep and loud breath.

"You don't have to—"

"No, it's not a secret or anything. You know how some people have this need to find out what kind of person they are by moving to the city and overcoming all the obstacles in that environment? The high rent, the pollution, the crime, the competition for the jobs available, moving from that one-bedroom apartment to the two-bedroom and on and on. Status this and who-you-know that and proper tips for proper perks and dress codes and having all the latest technology and fashion—"

"Yes," she said with a laugh, "I do know."

Frank giggled.

"Oh, so you can laugh?"

"I can. And I can sometimes go on and on." He kept his smile for a moment. "Anyway, before being so rudely interrupted, I knew that that wasn't the path I needed in order to find out who I really am. My path to understanding needed to be more introspective, and the north gives one plenty of opportunities for desolate, quiet, and uninterrupted introspection." With that, Frank finished his beer.

"And what have you discovered?"

"That can only be revealed with another round. Want me to grab you another?"

"Sure."

It was comforting to hear another person have a similar perspective, an appreciation for solitude. And for just half a second, Guin thought Jacob her Richard and Frank her Eugene, following right along in her mother's footsteps by dropping the companion, Richard, and moving on to the man who understood and accepted her, Eugene. Hadn't some psychologist said that all girls end up marrying their father and all boys their mother? Well, that hadn't been the case with Shirley, but, for that split second, it was making sense to Guin.

As she stepped outside the wheelhouse, she woke the wind, which embraced her in its icy grip and made her shudder. She flipped her hood up and turned her back on it, then watched the large snowflakes race down diagonally to the black water surrounding her. Then a gust strong enough to push her forward and make her throw her hands up on the cold metal wheelhouse frame brought with it the odor. It grazed her face for just long enough to confirm it wasn't her imagination. It was a bit more earthy this time, like damp leaves and other vegetation breaking down in a compost heap, but it still held that bitter ozone bite that made her cover her nose. Another gust! It wasn't the frigid air or the smell that made her spine quiver this time. With that gust came a noise, some soft and alluring voice that uttered a single word: "Guin." At least that's what she thought she heard. At the same moment, Frank emerged from below and rushed to her, pulling her inside.

"Geez! It feels like it dropped another ten degrees since I went down," he said, handing her a Molson.

While she knew that he'd probably have the same answer as the previous night, she asked anyway, "Did you smell anything odd out there?"

"I don't think I even took in a breath." He took a sip. "Didn't you think you smelled something last night?"

"I must be really sensitive to smells."

"And back at Fort Chip as well. I suppose there are some odd odors that pass from time to time. Between the forests, bogs, and even all that mess down Fort McMurray way, it all catches in the wind to some degree." He opened the wheelhouse door and breathed in a deep lungful of freezing air. "I don't notice anything odd at the moment."

It happening two nights in a row didn't seem like it was all in her head. There was something emitting that odor and the others weren't picking up on it. Not wanting to press it, she said, "I guess I really needed another beer," and laughed.

Frank closed the door, seeming satisfied that he didn't need to pursue it further. After Frank moved in and leaned against the window, they were now just a few feet apart.

"So?" she said, eyebrows raised.

"Um . . . "

"What did you discover?"

"Right, yes," he replied, letting himself smile again.

He did have a nice smile. And while he had seemed to not want her to be alone, starting conversations with her and doing things for her, Guin sensed that he would not be offended if she asked him to leave her be. She could also see in his guarded but excited expression that he was glad to be talking to someone. Guin also felt that she wanted to pay attention to his words, that there was something about his demeanor and magnetism that drew her in and kept her attention, even if he was only talking about the mundane.

"I discovered that it takes a certain kind of person to make it in northern Canada. The Dene are rooted in the area, it's home to them, but others, like me, like Berin, and like you, we must possess some kind of deep-seated connection, some kind of understanding within ourselves and our environment that allows us to be okay here." He shook his head. "I might not be explaining that well. What I mean is, most people I know don't do well outside society. I feel as though I've reached a true understanding of who I am by being outside of society, and I wouldn't have found the inner peace that I have had I stayed in Banff."

"You sound like a Romantic."

"I don't follow."

"Capital R." Shit! She didn't want to ruin the conversation by turning it literary, so she tried to keep it simple. "If you've heard of William Blake or Wordsworth, Percy Shelley—"

"Oh, yes, sorry. The Nature guys."

Guin wanted to clarify, but kept it pleasant. "Yeah. In tune with Nature."

Frank paused, then said, "It does make sense. Banff had a lot of Nature, but it wasn't until I came up here to be with Berin that I grew comfortable with it. That I considered *it* society, my society." He scratched his head involuntarily. "Does that make sense?"

It did make sense. It's not how she would have described it, not exactly her experience once she'd stepped foot off the plane back in Yellowknife for the first time, but it was close enough. "It does," she said. "It makes a lot of sense."

"And, I suppose, whenever I move on from here to start that new chapter, I can take that understanding with me."

They both had their backs against the wall, standing side by side, but Frank turned to Guin, resting his shoulder on the window now.

"I'm just not sure where that new chapter will be. Or when it'll be." He took another swig. "If Berin's able to get some kind of closure on this . . . expedition, it's possible we'll both be ready to move on." He met Guin's eyes now. "And if he gets closure, I'm not sure he'll still need me tagging along, so I'll have some big decisions to make. This fishing tour gig, while easy and peaceful, just isn't my endgame."

Frank stopped talking then and held her gaze. Guin stayed silent as well, peering into Frank's enlightened eyes. They'd made a connection, and the next step was forbidden, but Guin cast aside that vow and kissed Frank's chapped lips hard, putting her hand on the back of his head and pulling it toward her. A break for breath, then she kissed him a second time.

Frank let her do this without resistance, but he didn't take action of his own except to purse his lips and kiss her back, shoulder still against the window, arms slack at his sides. She could feel him breathe in her scent, one that couldn't be perfume or deodorant, only the pure and natural aroma of a woman, a far more primal scent that didn't stimulate olfactory senses and begin firing neurons as if he'd breathed in some body spray or Chanel No. 5; rather, she knew that it had fired in his amygdala and had sent shockwaves directly to his groin as it throbbed against her through his jeans.

When Guin pulled away, she felt liberated and let out a deep breath. The look on Frank's face, that bewildered and yet ravenous look, made her say, "Sorry," but not really mean it. Well, she did mean it, but not for the kiss. She meant it because she knew that it was as far as it could go under the circumstances.

"Don't be," he said.

"Okay." Guin took a sip of Molson. "I won't."

CHAPTER 5:
STONY RAPIDS

i

"SO JUST HOW cold does it get around here?" asked Edmund.
"Well, as you've seen the past few days," said Berin, "we get above freezing at times and then dip below at other times. It's usually November before it stays below freezing."

"I mean at the coldest times."

"It can get in the negative thirties."

"Is that Fahrenheit or Celsius?" asked Edmund.

Berin smirked and took a drink. "When it's that cold, it doesn't matter. If you'd waited a few more months, you'd be driving across this lake rather than chartering."

Even saying the words caused Berin's chest to revolt and send a charged pain to his heart. The timing *was* right. Berin could feel it all the way in his bowels. Had this group waited until Lake Athabasca had frozen over, Berin might be doing it all alone or possibly just giving in to grief and ending it all. But, now, he was determined to uncover every stone that might hold a clue to the disappearance of his Julia until his body no longer had the strength to do so, and he'd be on this journey with others seeking similar answers.

As these thoughts jolted through Berin's mind, he saw Guin get up and climb the narrow steps to the snowy deck. Noticing Frank hop up to join her made him smile a rare smile. Once they'd both disappeared, Berin eyed Eugene and Edmund.

"Eugene, I know why you're here," said Berin, turning his gaze to Edmund, "but, you . . . I don't buy that it's some unknown unfinished business." With his bottle of beer in hand, he pointed to Edmund. "It's just the three of us now, two of which are here for obvious reasons. So, tell."

Edmund took a deep breath and shifted his attention to the floor before responding, his eyes darting between Berin and Eugene. "I don't know that my explanation will give much more clarity than what I said earlier."

"Try us," said Eugene.

After a brief pause and a loud exhale, Edmund confessed, "I went back to Saskatoon with the remains of whatever they found out here and told the authorities everything that I knew. They did their tests and confirmed that I was not a suspect at the time. So, I went back to Chicago. But, when I got there, it wasn't home. Before this job, I was whole and considered Chicago my home . . . that's where my roots are, deep and firm. Going back after all that, it was foreign as if I was an imposter, an interloper." His gaze now met Berin's. "I felt like I was a trespasser in my own city . . . in my own home." Edmund turned to Eugene. "After a few days of that, I called you." He nodded and finished his beer. "And here I am," he said.

"That's good enough for me. And Berin," said Eugene. "You?"

It was, but Berin didn't want to respond too quickly, so he finished his beer in a long gulp before responding with, "It is." He tossed his bottle in the bin and said, "Another round." It wasn't a question, so he didn't wait for a response before pulling three bottles of Molson from the refrigerator and handing one to each.

"I'm going to get us to Stony Rapids tomorrow, and our real journey will begin," said Berin.

Frank re-emerged from above and grabbed a few beers of his own. Berin met his brother's serious demeanor with a nod, but Frank didn't have a significant response, just a nod of his own before heading back up into the snowy night.

"I hope that the snow doesn't cause it to be too difficult," said Edmund. "It's so sudden how the weather shifts up here. When we were here, it was in the fifties . . . Fahrenheit," Edmund said with a laugh, receiving silence in return.

"When we get to Stony Rapids," said Berin, "don't let that feeling of not belonging make you hesitate or second-guess why you've returned. This is a large area, plenty of pockets to keep things hidden, but we're going there to shine light into those dark recesses." He was making eye contact with Eugene now. "And what we see might not be pleasant, but we've got to see it, internalize it, and move on. It's the only way. If we don't, then we'll probably not be making the return trip."

Berin knew that he was saying this for their benefit. He knew that he'd not be going back, that this was his final expedition. Deep down, he knew that Julia was dead, and the only comforting thought that had entered his mind since she went missing was that he'd be able to join her. That moment a few years ago when he'd screamed her name on Highway 964, he knew that he would not see her again, but that wasn't the point. The point was not giving up on one's soulmate. Julia was his love, and he wasn't able to give up on the slightest possibility that she was still alive, somewhere out there in that vast wilderness. And, until he had some physical and scientific proof that she was gone, he'd maintain some level of hope. For Berin, that meant full hope, to return the wedding band to her and tie together two lonely halves to make a whole, and he was willing to sacrifice his life for this. He was willing to die to know her fate, no matter how horrific, no matter how optimistic. The only way he'd stop hoping and stop searching was with something firm, and that hadn't been given to him yet.

The two men sitting across from him sobered quickly and nodded. They knew the risks and implications. They knew them the moment they'd stepped onto the Cessna Skyhawk in Hay River, then the taxi in Fort Chip. So, the only obstacle left was getting there, to Stony Rapids, which they did the following day without incident albeit with worsening snow.

ïi

The sleepy hamlet of Stony Rapids came into view shortly before noon. What caught Guin's attention after she stepped off the trawler and onto the snowy dock was not the absence of human life or the odd silence. It was the barbed-wire fence that separated the dock from the parking lot. Impaled upon the barbs were two small mice, one still and the other upside down, legs flailing, blood dripping and burning a red hole in the white snow below. She approached them slowly, inquisitively, not really knowing what to make of this cruel display. Guin stared at them for what felt like a long time until Frank's voice broke the trance.

"Shrike," he said.

"What?"

"A shrike did that."

It was a word she hadn't heard before. Was it something mixed in with the folklore of the region or some myth?

"It's a bird. I'm surprised they're still this far north this time of year."

"A bird?" No, it wasn't a bird. Torture was a human thing.

Frank smiled, looked up toward a nearby tree, and pointed to it. "There it is. The butcher bird of the north."

When Guin turned and saw it, a light breeze followed. The bird was small, its cry a muffled trill. With oily black eyes, a gray head, and a band of black across its face like a domino mask, it loomed over them, gripping the tiny limb, its head swaying back and forth like a cobra. Her eyes blurred for a moment, making her realize she was staring.

"They're hanging around for the unexpected feast," a male voice said.

Guin met the stranger's kind but tired hazel eyes as he opened the gate.

"Unexpected?" said Frank.

"Yeah, everyone left a little over a week ago save a few souls." He approached Frank with his hand out. "You Berin?"

"No." He shook the man's hand. "Frank, his brother. This is Guin."

Releasing his grip, he said, "Joe Simpson," then nodded toward Guin. "Ma'am. Snowmobiles, fuel, and the other supplies you requested are up and around the corner. Walkie-talkies with new batteries. Your cells won't work in many parts, but these have a distance of about fifty kilometers as long as there's no interference like hills or mountains in the way." He began gesticulating as he continued, an odd expression on his face. "I don't want to sound portentous or anything, but, be careful out there. If something happens, you might be on your own for a while, so I added some extra batteries, a few more items to the first-aid kits, and some extra provisions. And—"

"Joe," said Frank with a nervous smile, "why did everyone leave? I thought this place would be filled up for the last few days of bear season."

"I don't even try and begin to understand why the locals do what they do. But, I'm following suit. You'll find two RCMPs and a handful of volunteers who agreed to stay back and keep an eye on everything, make sure to put out any fires and keep an eye on the power. Stuff like that." He glanced at the mice, both motionless now. "And these poor bastards," he said with a smirk, "they've been wandering all over the damn place, getting picked off by your friend up there and everything else. That's one way to take care of a mouse problem . . . desert the town."

"How many people are usually here?" Guin asked.

"Little over two hundred." Pointing to the impaled mice, he said, "So, you'll be seeing a lot more of that while you're here."

"Wonderful," said Frank. To change the subject, he added, "We'll all be inland except one. He'll be staying on board, so don't worry if you see someone over here."

"Noted."

...

III

They loaded the snowmobiles and departed, taking Robillard Street to the Highway 964 intersection, Edmund in the lead position. Highway 964 would take them all the way down to Black Lake, but Edmund didn't turn right on to the highway; rather, he kept going straight, the road narrowing considerably. At this, Berin honked the horn, a pathetic and almost whiny sound, but it did the job. Edmund slowed and finally stopped.

"What route is this?" asked Berin.

"It follows the river a little ways, then it's wilderness. Our camp was a few kilometers past the end of the road. That's where we're going as a starting point."

Berin nodded, then got off the snowmobile. "Will you all meet me where the road ends? I need a moment."

"Sure," said Edmund.

All but Frank pushed on. When they had all disappeared around the next curve, Frank approached him and asked, "What's going on?"

"I didn't know about this road." Berin could feel his heart begin to race, blood pressure rising. "I didn't know it was here, Frank!" When Berin had been here before, he had flown in. From the airport, the road intersected with 964. To the left, it passed the turnoff to the health authority and went up to Robillard, which he thought was a curve back into Stony Rapids, not an intersecting road that would take him along the Fond du Lac River.

Frank only stood there. There were no words he could say.

"I walked the length of that highway all the way down to Black Lake, but I didn't think to check in the other direction."

Berin eyed Frank now, tears welling up in his eyes. "I thought it just went to the health authority. I didn't know it intersected. This place is so small, I didn't think there'd be more." The adrenaline shifted to anger as he realized that he wasn't the only one. "Why didn't anyone else say anything? They fucking live here and would have known. Why didn't they say anything, Frank?"

Berin realized that he'd grabbed Frank's jacket and had it in a death grip before letting it go.

"I'm sorry, Berin."

"She could have been taken down this road. She may not have even gotten started toward Black Lake." He paused, teeth clenched, cheeks damp with melted snow and warm tears. "All that wasted time."

He sat in the snow, shoulders slumped and feeling defeated.

"But what about the ring, Berin? You found it down the highway. Doesn't that lead you to believe that your search was at least in the right direction?"

"It could have been planted there . . . I don't know." He let out a deep breath, the air clouding around his covered head. "I may need to stay back, Frank. Take the route at a slow pace and see if I recognize anything."

"Berin, there's a foot of snow on everything. There'll be nothing to see."

"At least I'll know that I tried, Frank!" He exhaled a labored breath. "Go with the others, and I'll catch up with you. I'll get your location with walkie-talkie. It shouldn't be more than a few hours."

"I don't want to leave you, Brother! Let me help you."

"You've helped me for two years, Frank. By coming along, you're helping me again. So, please, help me how I need you to help me now. Go with the others. I have to do this alone, just as I did back then."

"God damnit! Fine. But, if you're longer than two hours, I'm coming back for you. That's the only way."

Berin got to his feet again. "Deal." He hugged his brother, then watched him get back on the snowmobile and disappear around the curve.

The anger and sadness dissipated, replaced with an eerie tinge of déjà vu. This time, snow fell at an increasing pace, but the sense of urgency was the same. As if her disappearance had just occurred. Berin didn't waste any more time. Instead of walking, he got back on the snowmobile and let his senses, his instinct, guide him as he moved along at a snail's pace. There had to be something here, even if it was just a feeling. The highway down to Black Lake left him with only a tiny clue. This had to be different! It was the only route he hadn't investigated.

"I will find you, Julia." He wanted to yell her name as he had done so back then, but he knew it was moot. So, meter by painful meter, he plodded along, waiting for any sign, for anything . . .

iv

The end of the road came quickly, a mere ten-minute ride, then they were fully off-road into the Canadian backwoods where there were no more houses, no more signs letting them know where they were, and no more human inhabitants. It was the wilderness, a swift river on one side, dense and dark forest on the other, amid snow and falling temperatures. Another ten minutes at this rate and Guin would be in the most remote place she'd ever been, for her camping trips from Yellowknife didn't take her more than a kilometer from civilization. But it wasn't ten minutes, it was approaching forty-five before Edmund stopped his snowmobile and stood. On one side, the Fond du Lac River raged, a thunderous roar of frigid whitewater crashing on boulders, walled on both sides by willow bushes, not the peaceful waters back at Stony Rapids dock. On Guin's other side, a wall of spruce and alders collected more and more snow as it fell, lengthening the shadows cast by those giant trees.

"This is where our camp was," said Edmund. "Woodcock Rapids. This is the last place I saw them."

CHAPTER 6:
THE THING IN THE WIND

i

THIS IS THE *last known place my mother has been*, thought Guin. It wasn't much different from the landscape in her beloved Yellowknife. She had the perverse thought that her mother was lucky to have been in such a place when she died, that Guin could only hope for such a place to pass when her time came. But, the thought was quickly squashed with guilt. Why would she think such a thing rather than trying to hold on to that sliver of hope that her mother was still alive?

It was difficult to move around in the thick snowsuits, but they got the camp set up in just thirty minutes, Edmund clearing a space in the center and getting a fire going before putting up his own tent. Guin would share a tent with her father, Berin and Frank would share, but Edmund would be alone. Once the small logs had burned down to embers, Edmund put a pot of water on for coffee at the same time Berin's voice came through the walkie-talkies asking for their location. Guin overheard Frank tell him, no questions asked. But that was not the case when Berin arrived. He was despondent, dejected. The man looked like he'd slit his own wrists. Thank God he had to share a tent with his brother.

Eugene sat in the snow outside their tent as Guin approached him and said, "Dad, how are you holding up?"

Stoically, he said, "Fine. I'm fine. You?"

She nodded, but she knew that he wasn't fine as much as she knew that she was not fine. Something about being in the last known place her mother had been seen alive sent shimmers of sadness and guilt through her being. But it wasn't all bad. The bank of the Fond du Lac River was only a stone's throw away. This natural waterway reminded her of her lake, but that was not what grabbed her attention and calmed her nerves. It was the thicket on the other side of it that did that. The wall of spruce and jack pine seemed darker over there, not holding as much of the falling snow as those on her side of the river. It took her back to her mother's words about her sanctuary back in Tennessee, that copse of trees that meant so much to her. The same one that had been cut down and turned into a highway not long before she fled that oppressive family and oppressive religious state to pursue her life, her passion. For her sweet mother to have probably died out here was almost like bringing her home, like the hymns say, easing her from this life to the promised land.

Her thoughts were washed away by a heavy gust of wind that stole out from across the river, investigated the camp, then whistled its way through the massive maze of trees. There must have been something dead across that way, the odor of rot mixed with the gust, and then it went away. It was calm again. The snow falling lazily again. Guin had to clean the snow from her glasses for the hundredth time.

"Coffee's ready," said Edmund.

"Edmund," said Eugene, "can you take me through it? Now that we're here, can you go through what happened?"

"No, that will not be helpful." Edmund poured coffee in his mug, the steam so dense it was as if there was a tiny fire in his cup. "What is helpful is that we're all here."

"I don't follow," said Eugene.

Guin noticed Berin's attention focused on Edmund now, the yellow fire reflecting in his eyes as he stared at him from across the flames. It wasn't a malicious stare. No. Just curious.

"Something happened out here that I can't explain." His eyes met Berin's now. "Many things happened," drawing out each word, "out here that can't be explained. And . . . " His voice faltered, but he caught it and regained control after a painful-looking swallow. "And I need to know." He looked at each person at camp, fixing his gaze on each for a second before moving on to the next. "We all need to know."

As if on cue, a small shrike flew over their camp, then swooped down and landed on one of the tents. It glanced down at all of them, chirped out a few innocent sounds, then flew off into the forest.

"What is it that we need to know, Edmund?" asked Frank.

"I can't really describe what happened. I can't really describe how I felt. It's just something that you have to experience on your own, which is why I needed us to start here."

ii

The temperature dropped with the sun as a steady breeze kept the campfire low and flickering. The plan was to start fresh in the morning now that they'd made it to the camp. They'd be the investigators, hoping to find something the RCMPs didn't turn up. Hoping to find anything at all to give them closure. Berin and Edmund had each gone inside their tents, Guin's father finished doing his business behind a tree and entered their tent. That left her and Frank sitting at the dying fire. They both knew there'd be no privacy here, not like there was back on the boat, but the mood had shifted so much that privacy wasn't on their mind.

For Frank, it was simple insomnia that kept him at the fire and reaching for his flask, the only sleep aid he believed in. For Guin, it was fear that she couldn't quite put her finger on. If she could stay awake all night and not be fatigued in the morning, she'd choose to do so, but she had to be alert and useful. So what was it that made her sit there, staring at the flames licking the remnants of a thick branch? To sit there and continue shivering as snow blew in her face and iced up her glasses?

Frank didn't dare break her concentration. He was smart enough to know that she wasn't thinking about him at that moment and that his intrusion would be most unwelcome, so he just sat there as well, taking several long draws from his flask and hoping its effects would happen sooner than later. But what happened next sent an unwanted and undesired chill down his spine that no amount of Canadian whisky could warm. He'd tilted his head back while taking a long pull, enjoying the burn of the whisky as it coated his throat. When his eyes were level with Guin again, he saw her staring at him with an expression that he could only describe as pure fear, as if there was some horrifying creature lurking behind him and she was frozen in fright. The first image that crossed his mind was a bear. Hadn't they been talking about bears with the guy back at the dock? Was there a bear behind him?

"Guin," Frank whispered, "what's behind me?"

She didn't seem to register his question or anxiety.

"Guin," he said in a louder tone.

Still no response.

It rattled him. He could feel the heat rising, his armpits immediately sweaty, gloves quickly becoming damp. There *was* something behind him, something that could cause him harm. Frank did the only thing he could think to do. His fight or flight instinct kicked in, and he leapt to his feet, swirled around, and was met with a wall of gigantic trees.

What the hell!

"Frank," Guin said.

He turned to her and repeated his thought verbally.

"What?" she asked.

"That look you gave me, like there was something behind me!"

Guin shook her head and repeated, "What?"

"God damnit!" he said, rubbing his forehead. "What were you looking at just before this? You made me think there was something behind me."

She wore a very confused expression in response. Not the artificial kind that Frank had seen with certain annoying tourists back in Banff, but genuine. The kind that couldn't be mistaken for anything else.

"I'm sorry," he said. "I just got a little freaked out."

"It's okay. I just had déjà vu, that's all."

He sat back down, then said, "About?"

A loud pop came from the pathetic little fire causing Guin to pause for a moment before shaking her head and saying, "Nothing important or interesting."

He knew better than to press a woman who gave an answer like that. What that meant was either the literal meaning or it meant that she didn't want to involve you and don't you dare press it. So, he didn't.

"I think I'm going to try and get some sleep," he said instead. "If you want me to stay out with you, I will—"

"No, no. You go ahead. I'm fine."

And he did go ahead, not understanding the strange direction the night had taken. And, further, not wanting to have another moment of unnecessary fear.

As Guin watched Frank disappear into his and Berin's tent, she recalled her epiphany. This place, this camp where her mother had disappeared, it was familiar. No, not familiar. She'd been here before. In fact, she'd been here several times. But, how could that be possible? Guin knew that she wasn't mistaking the place for some camping site she'd been to when she'd taken a weekend for herself up in Yellowknife. But, if not that, then what?

Her gaze went back to the fire, its flame going from diminutive to gone now, leaving behind glowing embers. She took off her glasses, causing her vision to get slightly blurry, but clearer without the snow and ice building up on the lenses. Guin leaned in toward the campfire, feeling the welcoming warmth of the hot coals on her face while the back of her neck burned and stung with the iciness of the snow and wind, that stinging feeling more like a hot coal on her skin than her cheeks and forehead, which were closer to the actual heat.

And then a pang. It pulsed in her gut and that part of the spine that connects to the skull. It was the kind of pang that tells you that you're being watched. Guin hadn't felt this before, but she knew instinctively its meaning. She made a point to not be like Frank and make any rash moves. Instead, she stood slowly, a tingling emerging at each vertebra, before turning gradually around. Unlike Frank, she *saw* something. Something that answered her lingering question. It was a large moose standing and staring at her from across the river. At least she thought it was a moose, for the snowfall was dense, the wind brisk, and her eyesight impaired. After a moment, a terrible gust sent blinding snow toward her, knocking her down. She glanced at the tents to be sure the gust hadn't compromised their supports, then her focus was skyward toward the moonlit clouds dropping masses of snow. And when the snow unexpectedly shifted for a second as if a controlled gust shot through it all just a few meters above her, there was a distinct shift in atmospheric pressure, as if bearing down on her a great invisible weight that seemed to pin her down into the snow. With it, a strange odor, sweet and pungent like ozone, filled her chilled nostrils, and it gave her clarity.

It was the dream! She was living a version of that damn dream that her mother had written about. The boy, Max, he hadn't stumbled into a glade or ice-covered lake, he'd reached the river's edge after it had frozen over. She'd seen the great moose from the dream! She'd felt it as it exploded into its own personal snow gust, but here, there was that distinct smell that accompanied it, that stench of ozone that hadn't been present in the dream. *People can't smell in dreams*, she thought, remembering that from some article or documentary. She hadn't been taken like Max. She'd remained an observer. But, now, that dream had stepped into reality. There was no abrupt ending by waking up and going on with life as usual. This was life now, the dreams a mere training, a slight bit of clairvoyance to help better prepare for the obstacles ahead.

As Guin lay there, sensing the invisible thing pass above her, the odor gone as quickly as it had come, she wondered about Max. There was certainly no Max here. And *she* wasn't Max because she hadn't been taken. So, if this was indeed *the* dream happening in reality, wouldn't there be a screaming young boy being taken away? She didn't know. It could have happened already. Or it could be a premonition for what was to happen in the future. Guin just didn't know. But she tried to glimpse one last possible image, the shimmer in the sky, but there were no stars, and the snow was too dense to see the treetops. All she did know was that the wind retreated abruptly, the snowfall eased to drowsy flurries, and a massive feeling of lethargy swept over her. It was all she could do to crawl to the tent and get on top of her sleeping bag. The moment she lay her head down, a wave of exhaustion pulsed through her body, a dizzying fatigue that pulled her to sleep in under a minute. Just before passing out, she thought she heard her mother's voice call out her father's name. It was distant and hollow as if she'd only heard an echo.

iii

"Eugene!"

"Eugene! You up?"

"Eugene! We need you out here."

It was Berin's voice coming from across the camp. Guin opened her eyes and found the sleeping bag next to her empty. She shot up, immediately awake, but with a memory as foggy as her glasses. She felt her way to the front of the unzipped tent flap. The sunlight reflected off the snow and fully blinded her.

Finally taking her glasses off and cleaning them, she said, "Berin, what's going on?"

"Don't come out just yet. There's strange footprints around the camp."

She put her glasses back on. "A bear?" Seeing Berin shake his head, she could see Frank and Edmund near the tree line behind him. "Where's my dad?"

"He's not in there with you?" asked Berin.

His eyes unnerved her. She was up and out of the tent in a few seconds, her gear and boots still on from the night before.

"How long have you all been up? What time is it?"

"Just a few minutes." He put his hands out as she started forward. "Wait, keep an eye on the tracks. We're trying to figure out what's going on."

The tracks were indeed through the camp, deep and more pronounced than those she'd made last night, which were only noticeable now by tiny dips in the snow as if the wind had stirred and tried to erase her bootprints. These resembled those of a bear, but she couldn't be certain, and with the sun's blinding reflection, it was hard to see much at all until she retrieved her goggles from inside the tent.

"Are there any tracks from the tent made by your father?"

The question alarmed her because she only saw animal tracks, at least what she thought were animal tracks. They were certainly not human, not made with snow boots, and not an ungulate, which took moose or caribou out of the equation. These tracks were something larger, and she couldn't make out any intricate details because of the snow and the sun's reflection.

"Where do they lead, Berin?"

"Out there," he said, pointing to the tree line.

"Then, that's where we're going."

"It is," he said flatly, as if it were the only option.

Frank and Edmund walked back into camp.

"They end just past the tree line," said Edmund. "The wind must've blown snow over everything from there."

Why didn't she feel fear? Why was there a strange sense of calm in this revelation, in remembering the sight of the great moose across the lake last night paired with her father's disappearance this morning? Or had he disappeared? She couldn't recall whether he had been in the tent when she'd crawled in last night or not. All of the previous night's details were blurry from the moment Frank had stood up and thought something had been behind him. Had her father snuck off on his own while she and Frank were sitting at the fire? And, if so, why not at least leave her a note? She didn't put it past him to go it alone, a soldier on a mission behind enemy lines . . . It would certainly be easier to do so alone than with a full squad. It made sense.

Guin turned and peered into the tent, checking if any of his supplies were missing. His pack was there, his goggles, and the key to the snowmobile. He would have been wearing his other gear. And, still, no note. More alarming was that he'd left the walkie-talkie. That was the red flag. That was what made Guin certain that something was amiss.

"Frank," called Guin, "you saw him go to bed last night, right?" she asked, turning back around.

"I think so, right around when the others did."

"You were facing the tent, so you didn't see him get out at any point, even to relieve himself?"

"I didn't," Frank said, shaking his head.

"Edmund," Guin said, noticing the man had his back to her, staring at the tall evergreens caked with snow, swaying in the breeze, blue sky beyond.

"This might have been a mistake," he said, turning and facing her, "but I had to know." His chin quivered now as he forced out, "I *had* to know."

"Know what, Edmund?" she asked, noticing a concerned look on Frank's face and the blank expression on Berin's.

"When I was here before, there was no snow, no tracks like this, so I could only guess that something had been out there with us." He looked down at the tracks. "But, now, I know that something had been there then, and there's something among us now." He met Guin's eyes again, reclaimed control of his chin and voice. "We should go!"

As he said this, a series of dark thoughts passed through Guin's mind. She couldn't help it, and she certainly couldn't stop them from flooding in. A series of What Ifs? What if Edmund was behind it all? What if he had something to do with the disappearances of her mother and Annalisa and now her father? What if he'd only wanted to lure *him* out here? After all, he wouldn't have known that she was going to be along for the trip as well since her father had asked her the day before. And Berin, he and Frank insisted that they come along after they'd left Fort Chip. Was that it? Was

Edmund behind everything for some unknown reason? Maybe it was a secret obsession with her mother, and she rejected him so he killed her and decided that he'd have to kill Eugene as well, to somehow take the place of the man she loved.

But, then she remembered that faint sound just before falling asleep. While she couldn't remember seeing her father in the tent when she crawled in, she certainly remembered someone . . . no, not someone . . . it had been her mother calling out his name from somewhere deep beyond those trees.

"Guin!" said Frank, now standing by her side. "You're okay?"

Frank's voice stopped the thoughts that she couldn't, and Guin was thankful. "Yes, I am." Eying Edmund now, she said, "I'm not going anywhere. And neither are you. At least not until we find my father."

She was surprised when he didn't object. Maybe her thoughts were completely wrong. Wouldn't he want to flee the scene once he'd finished his task?

"We should pack up," said Berin.

"Do you think it's a good idea to radio Miksa and have him contact the RCMP about this?" asked Frank.

All eyes were on Guin now.

"I don't know," she said. "He may have gone off on his own. Maybe we should look first and see what we find." Even without his gear, Guin knew that her father could manage on his own. And, if it was indeed her mother's voice that she'd heard last night, maybe he was with her now.

"The tracks lead to the forest, so we should head into the forest," said Berin.

Those tall and dark trees loomed over them, swaying back and forth as if to say ominously "*Lasciate ogni speranza, voi ch'entrate* . . . Abandon all hope, ye who enter."

They left his snowmobile with the key, along with his pack and a note and walkie-talkie should he return to camp, then headed into the forest.

iv

It seemed as though they were entering another realm, a place where the elemental gods are worshipped and praised. What was once sunny, loud with the river's rumble, and blindingly bright was now dim and shadowed, calm, as if dusk had come early. The only noise was that of their snowmobiles, out of place and disruptive.

They had no official trail to follow, only the natural narrow paths the forest allowed. On either side, the jack pine interlocked with hemlock and trembling aspen, intertwining and unwelcoming. They had no clues along the way, but pushed forward in hopes that something would stand out. And something did after nearly ten minutes of slow travel. Guin spotted a cabin ahead and to the right. She signaled Berin before leaving the group and headed for the structure. When she got there, her adrenaline kicked in fiercely, so much so that her hands were shaking, and standing was difficult.

It wasn't just a huntsman's shack. This was large enough to live in. The windows were intact and the front door closed, but she didn't see any smoke coming from the chimney or any sign of footprints, so she didn't suspect her father was inside. Trying to maintain balance in the slick snow, Guin extended her arms and took baby steps to the door while the others arrived behind her. She knew that the interior would tell her if this was indeed the cabin from the dream. There was really only one thing that she was looking for, and when she peered in through the front door window, it was there, perched on the wall above the fireplace mantle, staring at her with its blank eyes. The moose head. This was Max's cabin. It was all real!

She tried the door, but it wouldn't budge.

"They looked here, but didn't find anything," said Edmund from behind her. As she turned to face him, he added, "Said that some family from Saskatoon owns it, uses it as a summer getaway."

"Did they say anything about the family?" she asked.

"No, just that."

Guin turned and put her gloved fist through the bottom right pane, the place where Max had watched his body contort in grotesque fascination. It gave with ease, and she reached in and unlocked the door.

"What are you doing?" asked Edmund.

"Wait out here," she said without turning around. "I just have to see something."

She closed the door behind her, took off her goggles, and scanned the front room. Sheets covered most items, but they did not cover the ever-present moose head lingering above the fireplace, its fur thick with dust. The cabin smelled unused, old. If a family had been using it as a summer home, they hadn't been here in years. Guin found it difficult to know whether it was indeed the cabin from her and her mother's dreams. Even though she'd had the dream practically every night for the past few weeks, her memory still had significant gaps the way memory often does with dreams. And the cabin hadn't been what she'd focused on anyway; it'd been the clearing, the boy, and that ominous shimmer up there atop the trees that warped the cosmos for a split second. It wouldn't be uncommon for any cabin to have a moose head on its wall out here. The uncommon cabin would be the one without the moose head, so she made quick work opening the doors and scanning the rooms to find nothing except more items covered in sheets, no sign of humanity, and no further recollections of or connections with the dream or Max, the boy. Even in the bedroom that would have belonged to him, she saw similarities in the view through the window. It would have indeed allowed moonlight inside, and, with the wind, made the shadows of the evergreens dance a hideous dance on his floor. But, when she turned toward the closet, there was no fear. Yes, it did have the darkness between the jamb and the slightly open door, but it was clear that there was nothing there. Certainly nothing to cause one to shiver. Leaving the bedroom, her eyes caught the sight of her past footsteps and how they were clearly the only prints made on that dusty floor in years, so she was satisfied and exited, taking one last look at that lonely bull moose head, staring back at her with its endless gaze. She might have lingered a bit more, but finding answers to where her father was outweighed finding answers to riddles from lucid dreams.

Outside, the others were on their snowmobiles waiting patiently.

"Nothing," she told them.

They continued searching, agreeing not to split up, heading east, south, back to the west, and north, only to backtrack and head back to the south surrounded by trees jutting up and stabbing the sky. Only a few bird calls here and there, probably the murderous shrikes seeking prey to torture. What they didn't find were tracks, human or otherwise. And after four hours of searching, zigzagging through the dense backwoods, checking the walkie-talkie, calling out Eugene's name every ten minutes, they ended up southeast of last night's camp as a frigid squall blew in gray clumps of clouds that dotted the sky.

As they started unloading and getting the tents set up, Frank said to Berin, "There's just nothing out here. If there was anything, it'd be covered in snow or taken by wildlife." Getting no response, he said, "We should contact Miksa now and have him report Eugene as missing to the RCMP back in Stony Rapids. And we should probably head back that way in the morning."

"I told you that I'm not leaving, Frank," said Berin. "I'm thinking clearly, just as you are, but I know that there's something out here that will give me closure. And I'm not leaving until I get that closure. You have to understand that."

"Explain it to me."

"I already have."

"Then do it again," he snapped. "Because what's happening out here is not okay."

"Frank, I need answers, and this is the only place where I can get those answers. Not back in Camsell and certainly not back in Banff. So, I'm here until then." He stepped closer to his brother. "You don't have to stay, Frank." Berin plodded through the snow toward the water and stopped when he was several feet outside their camp.

A sound came through the walkie-talkie, sounding like nothing more than static. Frank turned to Guin, who had already picked up her radio and turned up the volume.

"Hello," she said.

No response.

"Hello!"

Silence.

"Hello!"

Nothing.

"You heard it?" she asked the others, eyes on Frank.

"Just static," Frank said. "You heard something else?"

"I don't know," she replied. "I don't know what I heard."

Another squall, this one bringing with it the first batch of snow and gloomy, ominous clouds that blanketed the sky bringing an early night.

Guin tossed the radio into her pack and turned her attention back to her tent, silently, knowing only that she had to get her shelter up before the weather grew worse. Inside, she was confused. How was she supposed to feel with a mother missing and probably dead and a father who was now missing, both swallowed up by the very wilds that she'd grown to adore? Should she continue searching for him? Should she wait? Should she get the message to Miksa so that the RCMP could get involved? Or, should she just walk away from it all and go back to Yellowknife, letting fate handle everything? It was paralyzing! There wasn't a positive solution among the options, so she shook her head and tried to focus on the tent, but her body didn't obey. Rather, it revolted and not only caused her mental paralysis, but momentary physical paralysis as well.

"Berin," she finally called, "please have Miksa contact the RCMP."

Once she'd spoken the words, it was like oil applied to a long dried-out machine. She could move again. And once the tent was up, she climbed inside, lay back, and closed her eyes as snow pecked at her tent.

V

When Berin had seen the tracks back at the camp, he felt one step closer to closure. Julia hadn't disappeared somewhere along Highway 964. He would have at least sensed something back then. At least, that's what his gut had told him. No, she was somewhere in the dense forest between Highway 964 to the west, Stony Rapids to the north, Black Lake to the south, and the Fond du Lac River to the east, a region only inhabited by anglers and bear hunters a few months out of the year, and they typically stayed close to the shorelines, as they did now. The most hopeful moment he'd felt was when Guin had noticed the cabin. Something had ignited inside him, a sense of strange hope that Julia had somehow wandered through the forest, found the cabin, and decided to inhabit it. That she'd be in there, waiting for him to come and find her and return her wedding band to its proper place. Of course, the "why" behind such an action didn't make sense, but that had not been part of his motivation or curiosity. His only goal was to find her and hold her again.

As he'd watched Guin enter the cabin, he hadn't been able to move. His throat had tightened, stomach clenched, heart jackhammered the back of his chest. By the time he could move again, Guin had re-emerged and said that the place was empty. But was it? Should he have taken a look? Maybe it had to be him in there, and that would have been the only way she'd have shown herself. That they'd be reunited. Or if there had been a hidden door or space that Guin had overlooked, he could go through more slowly and deliberately so that if she had indeed not been there, there would have been no spot left unsearched. And who knew how effective those people in the search party Edmund mentioned had been. Maybe they'd just peeked in the windows and banged on the door.

"Berin," Frank had said, "she's not in there. Let's go."

So, he'd gone along with the group, choosing to be at the tail end to keep an extra close eye on everything around them, searching for anything that might be a clue, but there had been nothing, not even an instinct. The only feeling he'd had was the uncomfortable tinge one gets when they're being watched. And if that feeling was true, his gut told him that the eyes that were upon him weren't kind eyes.

At the new camp, Berin stood in shin-deep snow and stared out at the tranquil water of Middle Lake, a three-kilometer-wide swelling in the Fond du Lac River between Lake Athabasca and Black Lake, as chilled air crept down from Yellowknife. Even though the water was calm here, Berin could hear the rapids in the distance, its high-pitched sound like hard rainfall on concrete. A knot had formed in his throat that he struggled to keep at bay. All he wanted to do right now was drop to his knees, weep, and cry out her name like he had done on the highway, but he worked to keep it in this time. And every second that he forced it to stay down, the wind responded with growing vigor, its tempestuous howling erupting from the close-knit trees he'd recently emerged from, bringing with it a somber darkening of the sky and a warning of the chill yet to befall upon their tiny encampment.

"Berin," Guin called from behind, "please have Miksa contact the RCMP."

Her voice broke his trance, and he nodded, turned, and watched her disappear into her tent.

After his first attempt, there was nothing but static, as with the second attempt. It was possible that Miksa was asleep, but he'd been instructed to keep the radio close. So, when Berin tried a third time in vain, Frank practically yelled into the walkie-talkie, only to be met with the same level of static.

"Try mine," said Edmund.

Nothing.

Berin turned to Frank.

"He's probably sleeping," Frank said. "Man sleeps like the dead. Just try again in about an hour."

Frank was right. Miksa did sleep an abnormal amount of time, and waking him was next to impossible. But, Berin knew that there was something else. There had to be. Julia hadn't just disappeared, Eugene hadn't gone off on his own, Miksa wasn't just sleeping, and the radios weren't just out of range or having issues due to interference of mountains or weather. He also knew that Eugene hadn't come out here just to find answers and that Edmund hadn't agreed to join them for answers of his own, his unfinished business. No. Those two had come for the same reason. It was that invisible and strange magnetic force that pulled at their consciousness, that nameless thing that hadn't been assigned a word in any dictionary, only synonyms: addiction, passion, drive, faith, meaning, understanding, need . . . and so many others. It was the siren song that they could neither repel nor ignore. Berin knew this because that was the real reason why he was here, too. Yes, he needed closure on Julia's disappearance, but the dreams, the pull, the desire, the need! He resisted it as long as his body could muster, until reaching this breaking point. So, now he was here. His body eased, physically telling him that he was where he needed to be. And no matter what obstacles stood in his way, he was to push on and keep moving forward.

So, with Eugene missing, the radios not seeming to work, and no clues to fill in the blanks, Berin knelt down and pushed on, placing dry cuts of firewood in front of him and getting the fire started. It happened simultaneously, the fire's blaze roaring up to meet the roar of the north winds bringing thick snowfall at a gale's speed.

The whole experience was only bearable to those from the north. Berin and Frank had been up here for long enough to resist that spirit that dwells in the wilderness, seducing even the strongest of city folk into its clutches and keeping them yearning for those desolate wilds. Berin could tell in Guin's expressions that that spirit had seduced her by the way she reacted to the incidents back on the boat, and even her father's disappearance. She wasn't hysterical or demanding; rather, she pushed on with a demeanor of one who's under the influence, ignoring the potential dangers in favor of the desired outcome. But, he didn't know her exact desired outcome, and he wasn't going to pry, especially after hearing her tone and seeing her stoic expression just before climbing into her tent.

The temperature plummeted quickly, having lingered just below freezing through the day, low enough to freeze a bottle of wine. But it wasn't wine that Berin was drinking. He'd brewed tea strong enough to kill a man and warmed it up a bit more with Canadian whisky. Frank joined him, but Guin and Edmund hadn't emerged from their tents in the two hours since making camp.

"I'll fry up something for dinner if you're hungry," said Berin to Frank.

"I think I'll just have a little mix and jerky. Not much of an appetite." He said this while peering at Guin's zipped tent, then took in a mouthful of his tea. "Why don't you give me a bit more here, Brother? Hold the tea this time."

He did, filling Frank's cup halfway with Canadian Club and adding another splash to his own. The alcohol hit Berin more quickly than he expected, so he sat down next to the fire. Frank joined him, two lonely nomads huddled over licking flames.

"Berin, aside from the obvious strange circumstances, have you felt odd?"

"How do you mean?"

"I didn't want to say anything earlier with Eugene disappearing, but I've had this weird feeling like we're being followed."

Berin's eyes widened.

"I think Guin might be feeling it, too. Last night, after you all went to sleep, she scared the shit out of me. Looked at me like there was something behind me."

"Was there?" Berin interjected.

"No. I thought it might have been a bear or something like that. But since then, it's been nagging at me, that fucking weird feeling in the spine and the back of the head. Just gives me an overall feeling of unease. That's why I was hoping you'd consider heading back." Frank scanned the camp and beyond. He could see the tree line to his left and slightly out into Middle Lake on his right, but the snow kept them in a kind of fog, but one in which Frank felt others could see clearly inside but one that limited their view outside.

"I've felt it, too," Berin said. "And I wish I could leave here with you and the others, but I need more time." Even in the frigid wind and snow, the whisky warmed Berin's innards and loosened his tongue. He inched closer to Frank until they were side by side. "I need to tell you something, Frank."

Frank's jaw clenched, bracing for what sounded like very bad news.

"I already told you what the chief down in Black Lake explained to me, but I learned more." Berin gulped down the remaining whisky and tea from his cup, then poured in straight whisky to the halfway mark before continuing. "There is something bigger than us out here. Something that thrives in desolation. And when we, humans I mean, when we intrude, it responds. I think the McMurray fires were part of its response. The Fort Chip disappearances. That village of three hundred in BC that packed up and left overnight because one of the villagers claimed to have seen it nearby. Same way the folks in Stony Rapids and Black Lake left." He took another gulp. "You're right when you say that you feel like we're being watched, but it's no person doing the watching. We don't belong here. Julia didn't belong here. Edmund's team, I don't know. Considering the circumstances, I suppose they didn't belong here either." He finished the whisky now. "But, all of that being said, I'm still staying. Because there is that slight possibility that she's still out here somewhere."

Frank exhaled a deep breath, the cloud wisping away in the brisk wind. "How can that be?"

Berin's lips widened into a smile for just a moment before he replied, "Miksa knows why. And, in the morning, I want you to go back to the boat and let him tell you."

"Berin—"

"I mean it, Frank. I appreciate all you've done, but I think this last part needs to be just me." Berin stood, his head dizzy and legs unstable. A quick gust knocked him back to the snow. "Well, shit," he said, laughing for the first time in a long time. "Good night, Brother." With that, he crawled into the tent and fell asleep in just a few minutes.

Frank followed shortly after, having spent time alone by the dwindling fire. Part of him had wanted to stand watch, but the whisky had done its job. After a brief moment of calm and flurries, a squall had come from the direction of the forest carrying with it an odor that Frank couldn't pinpoint. It hadn't been like those out-of-place odors Guin had noticed back at Fort Chip. It had been something that seemed to straddle the line between known and unknown, belonging and not belonging, esoteric. And when it had passed a few moments later, the fatigue and alcohol having kicked in, Frank had mimicked his brother, crawled into the tent, and fell asleep.

"*Berin*," called a voice that was slow and drawn out as if struggling to shape each sound.

Berin woke the moment he recognized the voice, sitting up straight like a vampire might do. He scanned the tent. Frank lay next to him, his light snoring signaling that the sound did not come from him.

"Julia?" he whispered.

At this, Frank stirred. When he saw his brother sitting up and staring at the zipped tent flaps, he didn't say anything, just waited to see what was going on.

"*Berin*," she called again as a gust of wind slapped the side of the tent.

Frank noticed a change in the air. That odor. That pungent odor. And the strange shift in air pressure. When he swallowed, his ears popped as if he were on an airplane, and he could feel the atmosphere seeming to push down on him.

Berin knew that it was Julia's voice, but it was almost like a whisper, drawing out his name like some ghost from a horror film. It sounded like she was just outside his tent, keeping her voice low and deliberate so as not to wake the others.

Without hesitating further, Berin crawled forward and unzipped the tent and stepped out into the falling snow without his boots. The fire was a glowing circle of embers below, the blanket of clouds above glowing from a hidden gibbous moon above, his vision limited due to dense snowfall.

"Julia," he said again, this time in a normal tone, looking back and forth for any sign of movement.

Frank tried to sit up, but his bones felt heavy as if they were made of iron. He tried to call out to Berin, but his throat was dry and scratchy from the whisky and the cold.

When Berin looked down at the hot coals, he noticed the footprints again, the same shape and size as those back at the previous camp. It dawned on him that the tracks had to have been made very recently to be so pronounced in this heavy snowfall. It ignited his adrenaline and made him, in a jerky motion, shift his sight from one part of the camp to another to yet another. Whatever it was had just been there. It knew his name.

"*Berin*," came the voice again.

This time, it came from the thick forest, and his legs began moving toward it without his consent.

Frank kept trying to call to his brother, to sit up, to do anything that would break the trance, but he just lay there, paralyzed.

"*Berin*," came the echoey call again.

While Berin's body seemed to have a mind of its own, his actual mind didn't object. It was Julia calling him, after all. All he'd had to do was search in the right place and he'd have seen her and been reunited so much earlier. So many wasted hours and days in Camsell Portage that could have been bypassed had he only known about that unmarked road that headed east rather than the highway that took him south.

"*Berin*."

He was only a few feet from the tree line now. He looked down at the shin-high snow.

"*Berin*."

He kept walking, but he no longer progressed forward as his feet emerged from the deep snow.

"I'm flying," he said, then shot up into those glowing clouds, eyes going dark, consciousness fading and then leaving altogether, the last image being his socked feet above the giant spruce treetops.

Vi

Morning came with cleared skies and a fresh foot of snow on the ground. Guin was the first to emerge from her tent. The camp was not like the previous one. There were no prints in the snow or any signs of disturbance. The hot coals had endured the night's snow, and Guin added four dried split logs from her tent, putting them in a cross pattern atop the gray ashes. It took a few minutes, but golden flames were soon licking the calm morning air. A few minutes after that, she put the coffee on and sat back waiting for it to finish.

Across the campfire, she saw Frank and Berin's tent unzipped and Frank inside alone. He didn't look at her, just stared skyward without blinking. She trudged through the knee-deep snow to the tent and slid inside.

"Frank!" she yelled. *Oh, god, please don't be dead.* "Frank!" She shook him now.

"Ahhhh! Ahhhh!" he screamed, finally able to move again. "Jesus fucking Christ!" He bolted up, breathing heavy as if just finishing a marathon. "Berin!"

Guin nearly screamed as well, but just gripped his shoulders as best as she could with gloved hands. A sinking feeling filled her gut. It had happened again!

"Berin! Jesus fucking Christ, it took him! It fucking took him!"

"Frank! Frank, look at me. Tell me what you remember."

Frank sat there, his breathing slowly returning to normal before he was able to speak coherently. He turned his head to Guin, locking eyes. "She called for him. She called him out there."

"My mother?" she said without thinking.

Frank shook his head. "What? No. Julia. Julia called for him, but her voice was . . . odd."

"Like an echo?"

Frank's brow furrowed. "You heard it, too?"

"No, but I think the same thing happened to my father. I thought it might have just been my imagination or a dream, but, before I fell asleep, I thought I heard my mother's voice call out his name. But I dismissed it and fell asleep."

"It woke me. I saw him go out there, out to the fire, and then go off toward the forest." His chin began to quiver. "But I couldn't move, Guin! My whole body was paralyzed until you got in here and shook me. I couldn't fucking move."

"Frank, it was sleep paralysis. It's not your fault."

Frank didn't let the tears come. He gained control of his quivering chin, and she saw the moment the guilt and sadness left, leaving anger in its place. "Did you follow his tracks?"

"There's no tracks. The snow covered up everything."

"Shit," he said, letting out a deep breath. "You should check to be sure Edmund is okay."

Guin left the tent to get Edmund. When she returned a minute later, she saw Frank emerge looking contemplative. She could tell that something heavy lingered in his mind, but she didn't want to ask about it yet.

"Did you hear anything last night?" Frank asked.

"I didn't. I didn't stir until sunrise," Edmund said.

The unease, anxiety, and dread that she knew she should feel were absent, giving her pause for the first time on this trip. When her father disappeared, she had rationalized possibilities, but Berin's disappearance seemed to wipe those hopeful scenarios off the table. There *was* something far more sinister going on, and Guin felt neutral, almost numb. Yes, she gave the outward appearance of concern, but her heartbeat didn't shift and her breathing remained calm.

"What's going on?" asked Edmund as he joined them.

"Berin's missing now," said Frank, explaining to him the rest of the details.

"Jesus Christ."

"We need to go back to Stony Rapids and get the police," Frank said. "This is just too much."

Neither Guin nor Edmund responded, just stood there silently, eyes toward the blinding snow.

"Well!" Frank yelled.

Edmund nodded. "Agreed." He looked at Guin. "If we stay out here, whatever has them will just pick us off one by one, like before." He paused for a moment. "I'm sorry."

His words did shake her up a bit. The "whatever has them" part, as if her father and Berin were alive and being held prisoner. In that case, shouldn't only one of them contact the RCMP and the other two keep searching? The thought didn't linger too long. It was replaced with a morbid sense of understanding as she analyzed the actions, tones, and expressions of her two companions. They were feeling hunted, vulnerable, and defenseless. In short, easy prey. But, Guin didn't feel any of that about herself. While this wasn't her Yellowknife and her Great Slave Lake, she felt safer as one does when at home. That if there was anything out there, some being that had taken her parents and several others, she was either its equal or possibly superior, and the others had somehow found themselves beneath it, making them vulnerable. Of course, the sensible side of her knew that this kind of thinking didn't make sense. There was no hierarchical shifting of a species. Humans, *Homo sapiens,* were in one specific place or in another, but they couldn't be in two separate places on the same chart.

THE THING IN THE WIND

"If we leave within the hour," began Frank, "we shouldn't have any trouble being back in Stony Rapids before nightfall."

His words disrupted her thoughts, but she heard him loud and clear.

"We should get some coffee and breakfast in us beforehand," she said.

Frank nodded, then they began packing up all but a few provisions for breakfast. Edmund fried bacon, salmon, and the remaining eggs in a skillet over the hot coals, and they all ate ravenously, Guin taking most of the fish and ignoring the rest.

Frank was the first on his snowmobile. It wouldn't start. It wouldn't even attempt to start. Then it was Edmund. Same. Guin's snowmobile followed suit.

"Try Berin's," Edmund said.

Nothing.

When they examined the engine and battery of each machine, there were no tell-tale signs of tampering. The batteries were just dead. The machines were finished.

"So, what do you suggest we do now?" asked Edmund to Frank.

"Fuck!" Frank yelled, bellowing it out over the snow-covered bank of the Fond du Lac River and Middle Lake. He then let out an exasperated breath before saying, "We go on foot."

While he wore a dejected expression, Guin could see something else there. It wasn't fear. It might have been a strange mixture of relief, grief, and acceptance. But, she chose not to ask if she was correct. Instead, she emptied her pack of nonessentials and then slid it on her shoulders, ready for the trek.

"If we follow the river, it'll take us right back to where we started," said Frank.

"Lead the way," Edmund said. "It's the same thing that I did before."

They trudged silently through deep snow for nearly an hour without speaking a word to each other, until Guin broke the silence and said to Edmund, "What was the purpose of all this?"

"Excuse me?"

"The purpose of this. What did you hope to accomplish by coming back here? What did my dad really hope to find? And your brother. What did he hope to find?"

"Answers," said Edmund.

"Anything more than he'd found before," said Frank.

"It doesn't make sense. There are no answers to be found out here. Edmund, you're the only one that can help me make any sense of it."

"Me?"

"Yeah! Berin wanted answers about his wife's disappearance. My father wanted answers about my mother's disappearance. Frank's here because of Berin, and I'm here because of my father. Why are you here? It doesn't make sense to risk your life to attempt to find minuscule answers about the disappearance of a couple colleagues."

"Let me be sure I'm understanding you properly," Edmund said. "Are you accusing me of anything?"

Shaking her head, Guin said, "No! That's not what I mean. I just can't understand why you're here."

"I had nothing to do with any of this!"

"I'm not saying you did, Edmund! But, why are you here?"

"I didn't have a fucking choice, okay!" He let out a deep and exasperated breath. "I couldn't sleep, couldn't even close my eyes without seeing them. I had to come here because I feared that I'd not be able to sleep again."

With that, Edmund turned and kept trudging forward.

Guin acted as if she felt satisfied with his explanation and continued forward as well, but she knew that he was not telling her everything. It felt as though he was stalling, but, at this point, she didn't know what the point could be.

VII

The hike was arduous and slow, eating up massive amounts of energy in each of them. The rubbery sound the snow made as it was mashed down with each step was hypnotic, and they seemed to keep pace as if governed by a metronome, even though each step was heavier than the previous. Intermittent gusts didn't help because they always seemed to be walking toward them, like they were purposefully trying to slow them down.

Guin noticed ice forming on the river's edges, but it wasn't strong enough to endure the current, breaking off and melting with each swell of water from the approaching rapids.

They had been on the move for nearly five hours when Frank collapsed into the snow, his face skyward.

THE THING IN THE WIND

"What happened?" asked Edmund.

Taking in a few deep breaths, Frank said, "I'm exhausted. That's all I can do today."

"Understood," Edmund said, dropping down in the snow with him. "We should set up camp then."

Guin stood there, watching the two men. A morbid thought crossed her mind: *Which of you will end up missing tomorrow?* But, something else entered her mind as well. Why was Edmund so quick to stop for the day? It was only two in the afternoon? There was no suggestion to just take a break.

"Until we get back," started Guin, "at least one of us should be awake while the others sleep."

They both looked at her.

"It'd actually be smarter for two to be awake while one sleeps. Unless you want this party down to two."

Frank nodded. "Smart."

Edmund didn't respond. Instead, he started clearing a space for his tent close to the water where the snow wasn't as deep. And half an hour later, they had their camp, a triangle of tents with a small fire in the center, a small pot atop the flames to boil the water they'd retrieved from the river.

"Have either of you tried the walkie-talkie since yesterday?" asked Guin.

"Just a few minutes ago," said Edmund. "Nothing."

"Do you two mind taking first watch?" asked Frank. Shaking his head now, he added, "I don't know why I'm so exhausted. I just feel so heavy."

"Of course," Guin said. "Do you think you're sick? Running a temp?"

"No, I'm just tired."

"Okay." While she hadn't had the feeling herself, she knew that Berin's disappearance was weighing heavily on him. Guin couldn't relate. Her mother had been here doing what she loved. Her father, well, that hadn't fully sunken in yet, but he had been determined to find something that would give him answers, something that would help him make the mission successful. For those reasons, the weight of their disappearances was different, almost as if they hadn't disappeared at all; rather, had just gone away for a little while. That they'd return when they were ready and that she hadn't anything to worry about.

Frank lay down, keeping his tent unzipped, as Edmund joined Guin at the fire.

He poured boiling water into his mug, the aroma of strong black tea finding its way to Guin's nose.

"Tea?" he asked.

"No."

Putting the pot next to the fire, he sat in the snow, letting his impression make a frigid chair next to Guin's. As he did so, he fixed his attention on the shadows darkening the campsite, looked up, and watched more clouds approaching.

"You don't like me very much."

"I've no opinion of you, Edmund. I don't know you."

"Fair enough."

"But you should understand that I typically know when someone is keeping something important from me."

Their eyes met at this statement, and Guin clenched her jaw.

"I don't know—"

"Another lie," she spat. "Why are you here, Edmund? I'm not going to ask again."

She didn't mean it as a threat, but, after the words left her mouth, she quickly realized that that's exactly how it sounded.

"I . . . I didn't have a choice, okay!"

"You said that already."

He took in a deep, icy breath. "I'm here because I'm supposed to be."

This man had the appearance of a condemned person, wearing the kind of expression found on the face of an innocent man found guilty of murder. At least, that's what Guin thought of it. It was the first time she'd noticed that Edmund was here against his will and that he was scared. That was his dark secret: fear.

"Sorry. You don't have to explain," she said.

"I wish I had someone to explain it all to me. Since coming up here with your mother, I've been haunted. I don't even believe in all that shit, but I know that something latched on to me and hasn't let go."

Guin tried to be sympathetic, but Edmund was beginning to sound like some religious nut recently converted and trying to spread the gospel. *So much for trying to be understanding.*

"Haunted might be the wrong word, but it's the only one I know that can explain what's been happening. You have to understand, all of this happened without warning. We were just taking water samples. There were no fires from the locals to ward us off or bad weather to cause any delays. We were just here to help."

Guin listened intently now, feeling slightly embarrassed that she'd judged him so harshly, even if it was only in her mind. However, as Edmund continued arguing his case, a revelation sparked, and she voiced it before thinking about the implications.

"Why were the three of you here in the first place?"

"Testing—"

"No! This water doesn't flow out of Athabasca, it flows in. And last I checked, there's no tar sands around Black Lake." She stood now, and it took more effort than she expected. "So? What's your explanation to that one?" This man! Her emotions made another immediate shift, this time a mix of anger and a deeper suspicion. In her periphery, she made sure of the position of the pot of hot water in case he flipped and tried to lunge at her.

Edmund remained seated and calm, eyes shifting from hers down to the ground. "I wasn't the leader of our group—"

"That's not what I asked."

His shoulders slumped significantly now, head dangling like a marionette as he placed his hands over his face.

"Am I going to get a straight answer out of you today?"

"Shut up!" he yelled, hands dropping from his face and his menacing eyes glared up at hers. "Just shut the fuck up." He started getting to his feet.

Guin took a half step toward the pot, positioning herself beside it so that she could bend down, grab it, and fling the boiling water at him in one fell swoop.

Just three strides away from her, he yelled with his finger stabbing the air in her direction, "If you don't feel it, then you won't fucking understand." He stepped toward her, dropping his hands down by his waist. Two strides away now. He growled, "You're gonna die out here," with a grimace. "We're all gonna die out here."

"Step back."

"Fuck you! You don't call the shots here."

"Step the fuck back!" As her adrenaline rose, so did the wind behind her, carrying with it that pungent odor of ozone, making her wince and her eyes water.

"Fuck you," he said again, taking another step toward her.

And that was her cue. Guin turned and started to bend down to grab the pot, but Edmund was too quick. As if knowing her intention, he pushed her. It wasn't a violent push, just enough force to get her to the ground. And though her arms had been out to ease the fall, the snow was too deep to prevent her face from connecting and snow caking her glasses. In that instant, she expected more, expected him to either hit her or continue yelling, but there was nothing.

Guin rolled onto her back, took off her glasses, and rubbed the snow from her eyes. What happened next nearly put her in shock. There was rumbling behind her, the kind of vibration a train might cause, and a howl of terror bellowing from Edmund's mouth. There was nothing masculine about his cry, a soprano wail that one would expect from a frightened adolescent girl instead of a fifty-year-old man. A white flash, and Edmund's body lurched skyward in the grasp of what looked like a white-haired claw around his neck. It all happened so fast. Guin could only make out general details from her blurred vision, only able to conclude that a white thing had taken Edmund, but she knew that it had to be the same thing that had taken her father and Berin. That had taken her mother and Annalisa. That had haunted her and her mother's dreams for so many years. It was a thing, a mighty thing in the wind that had the power to shift stars.

She didn't know how to respond. Edmund was gone just like the others, and she'd seen the villain that had taken them firsthand. But, there was no screaming, no real fear. Just awe. She stared up at the clouds that began dropping snow, almost paralyzed in wonder, mouth agape. For the first time in her life, she knew what those churchgoers who had indoctrinated her grandmother and failed to indoctrinate her mother had felt while in their chapels. The overwhelming desire to worship something much higher than you. It burned through her, but she didn't give in, not even after getting a glimpse of the god she might worship.

"Guin!" called a voice. "Guin!" Louder this time. "Guin!"

She felt a hand on her shoulder now, her body shaking by its force.

"Guin!"

Guin finally broke her gaze and saw Frank above her, eyes wide, sweat beaded on his forehead.

"What's happening?" he asked.

She took a moment to answer, finally getting her glasses back on and seeing the world more clearly. Guin wanted to make sure that the words she spoke were the ones she intended to speak. So, getting back on her feet, she said in a direct tone, "Edmund's gone. And I don't know if we're going to make it out of here."

As Frank scanned the camp, Guin noticed his body grow rigid when he saw the prints in the snow, the same ones around the camp when her father had gone missing.

"It came back?"

Guin only nodded.

They were making eye contact now as he added, "Did you see it?"

She nodded again.

"What was it?" He was getting more and more agitated, more excited now. "What the hell was it?"

With a quick shake of the head, she said, "I don't really know. It was too fast."

"Too fast?"

"It was like the snow came alive, Frank. No, not the snow. The wind. It was like the wind came alive and took him away like a bird might do. Like one of those shrikes might do. Probably impaling him on a high branch somewhere deep in the forest." She took in a deep breath, then added, "It followed us here."

Frank didn't respond, just took in what she'd said.

"Edmund might have been right, you know?" Guin said, gazing at Frank deliberately. "We might not make it out of here."

"No," Frank said, shaking his head. "We are definitely getting the hell out of here. Together. You hear me?"

She nodded. "I hear you."

"How are you?"

"What do you mean?"

"I mean, should we just keep moving and say to hell with camp?"

The clouds coming in were darker, and they could see that they would bring with them far more than flurries, but Guin opted for them to keep camp one last night.

"I have an idea that's probably stupid, but—"

"Tell me."

"I think we should ride it out tonight and stay in the same tent, put some precautions in place, and push ourselves to make it back to Stony Rapids tomorrow. I don't think either of us could really make much progress today. You're exhausted physically, me mentally. We're going to need to be alert from here on if we want to get back at all."

"Okay."

"And it clearly doesn't matter whether one person stays awake or not. Nothing we do may matter if we're just being hunted."

Frank nodded.

"I know it's just a thin layer of fabric that barely keeps the elements out, but I feel that we'll be safe in the tent. The others were all outside when they were taken."

"Okay."

"Frank, what is it?"

"It's surreal. Of all the horrible things that have happened here, the thoughts going through my mind are scolding me about my response to horror films I watched years ago."

"What?"

"When I'd watch horror films, I'd always complain that the characters weren't reacting to whatever the antagonist was. You know, some ghost or demon or serial killer. But, I'm standing here, three out of five of our party, one my own damn brother, have been taken by what you're calling some creature in the wind, and I'm not losing my fucking mind. Then, you suggest that this huge creature will somehow be repelled by the fabric of a cheap tent. And you say it with a straight face, your voice doesn't falter an instant. So, I guess Hollywood got it right. I thought people should be going wild and screaming and acting like they're fucking nuts . . . or at least trying to rationalize what the supernatural element is. But, no. We're standing calmly in the middle of what will probably be a blizzard, many kilometers away from a desolate village, being hunted."

"Frank—"

"I'm fine. But don't think I'm falling asleep sober." With that, Frank climbed back into his tent.

Guin turned her attention back to the fire. Why had it gone after Edmund and not her? Something so powerful could certainly have taken both of them, but it only went after him. Again, why? And, even without the help from Frank's thoughts about Hollywood horror films, an even more pressing question on her mind was why she wasn't more shaken by it all. Instead, she had a weird sense of calm about the whole thing, even her father's disappearance. It just didn't seem real, like it had all been some dream, some ongoing nightmare, but it had no power because she knew that she was dreaming.

She thought about how Jacob would be taking it all had he joined them. The thought caused her to giggle for just a moment, knowing that he would have fit Frank's suspected description of one in such a situation, anxious and going a bit crazy. And it was this realization that solidified her decision to part ways with him. It hadn't been back on the boat kissing Frank; it was this stark contrast in frequency. She was in tune with what was around her, juggling her teaching obligations with her desires to be out in the wild, and being a wife in a relatively new home. He could only be a husband, a husband who loved his wife but hated everything else about his life. It didn't take a clairvoyant to know that his unhappiness would soon bleed into his love for her, so she would set him free. She had to. Not only for him, but for her. That moment, staring at the embers as the snow fell harder, Guin knew that she was to be independent, to be alone. If someone came along that fit, then okay, but, if that never happened, she knew that she'd still be happy. That she'd be okay at her lake, in her forest, her home.

It was with this decision and understanding that she climbed into Frank's tent and zipped them up inside.

...

VIII

When Guin entered the tent, Frank was swallowing a mouthful of whisky.

"Give me that," she said, then took a swig from the Canadian Club bottle. She screwed the cap back on the bottle and tossed it to the side. "We'll leave at dawn."

Frank was on his side, head perched up with this hand as he said, "Dawn it is." He cleared his throat, then added, "You not wanting me to put a bigger dent in that bottle?"

She shook her head while saying, "No."

And when she put her hand between his legs, his body tensed, member stiffening. Laboring a swallow, he then said, "A kiss is one thing—"

"Shut up."

The man didn't speak another word for the next hour, just let his actions do the talking. He kissed her deeply, her lips, her neck, her lips again. And while he kissed her, his hands worked to get her out of her snow gear, her other layers, and finally appreciate her underthings, keeping her panties and bra intact for now. Frank was almost surprised when he realized that she'd been doing the same thing to him, and he found himself in nothing more than his undershirt and briefs.

As his lips ventured south to her chest, her bra came off, and he spent a while there before going farther and making her moan involuntarily. His time there didn't last long, as she demanded him to be inside her, and he followed her orders, making love to this woman for nearly twenty minutes before finishing.

He was larger than she'd expected, growing inside her and meeting that line between pleasure and pain.

As they lay there, inside his single sleeping bag, two naked and sweaty bodies entwined, they held each other and fell into a deep sleep.

Guin was the first to wake, the morning sun illuminating the tent like a spotlight. In the night, Frank had rolled over, his back to her now. The scent of his hair, a mixture of sweat and the outdoors, gave her ease. She had no regrets. She didn't even feel like she'd done anything wrong. So, instinctually, she slid closer to Frank and put her arm around him, needing his warmth as the temperature was well below freezing. Frank didn't stir, and she was in no rush to get the day going.

In that moment, Guin wondered how life would be different with someone like Frank, a man who could handle the great north, could handle the desolation. And she wondered if she should attempt such a thing once all of this was over or whether she should just be alone, the only assured positive outcome.

As she lay there, a chill caused her whole body to shiver a moment. While she had contemplated her future with Frank, he had inched away from her in his sleep, so she scooted closer to him again, but this time his skin was cold like a corpse, not warm and comforting as it had been just a few moments ago.

What the hell?

"Frank," she said, gripping his shoulder and shaking him. "Frank," she said, louder this time because he hadn't stirred. "Frank!"

THE THING IN THE WIND

She yanked his shoulder toward her, turning him onto his back. His frigid body was white as snow, but his head was misshapen. Guin blinked rapidly, then focused. Yes, the man she had made love to and fallen asleep next to had gone through some hideous metamorphosis. Sharp teeth like a bear. Snout like a moose. Eyes black and reflective like the heartless shrike.

The transformation caused her to scream.

"Guin!" yelled Frank.

Her eyes closed, giving her nothing but blackness amid the deafening howl of her screams.

"Guin!" yelled Frank again.

When she finally opened her eyes, Frank was hunched over her, the sky clear and starry behind him. And dark. With a dry and scratchy throat, shivering body, and a mouth that would not produce words, only attempt such a feat, her mind realized that it was not morning at all, but still night. And she was outside. And she was so, so, so cold!

"F-F-Frank," she said, and she couldn't say anything more yet.

"Come on," he said. "Let me get you back in the tent."

What was she doing outside? Her eyes closed for a few seconds, and her mind tried to piece together what had happened behind frigid eyelids. But nothing. Her mind was blank after the memory of scooting closer to Frank. It didn't make sense. For the first time in her life, something had happened that she didn't recollect and understand. It made her question everything. What was real? What had really happened up until this point? Or was she still dreaming . . . or whatever she had been doing?

Guin looked down at her body. She was in the snow, nearly naked save her panties and bra. That alarmed her as well. If her memory served her correctly, she should have been naked.

Frank was still hunched over her, so she attempted to put her arms around him, but they were numb. *Am I paralyzed?* No. She could feel the cold, so that meant she wasn't paralyzed. Just numb.

"C-carry me."

He obliged, scooping her up with seemingly supernatural strength, taking her to the tent, and proceeding to get her in her snow gear, as if he'd done it a hundred times.

"Let's get you warmed up," he said. "I'll get the fire up."

It didn't take too long for her arms to work again, and she pulled on her remaining gear. She watched Frank get the fire blazing in only a couple minutes, placing two cut logs in a cross, then stacking several atop them, leaving plenty of room for oxygen. As it started roaring, she left her tent and huddled near the flames. The heat was intense and inviting, giving her the warmth she thought she'd had against Frank earlier. She had been so cold that she feared that she'd get too close to the flames, but she had no need for alarm.

Frank disappeared into his tent for a few moments before joining her at the fire. Lighting a cigarette, he said, "Why the hell did you come out into all this in your underthings? Moreover, why were you just in them at all?"

Guin didn't answer immediately. Her attention stalled while focusing on the red glow of the cigarette end as Frank took in a long drag.

"I don't have an explanation, Frank."

Frank's skin glowed in the flickering firelight, eyes almost like a strobe light. "Well, why do you think?"

Guin couldn't determine what had been dream and what had been reality. At what point had everything turned into a dream? Not letting embarrassment get the best of her, she asked, "What's the last thing you remember?"

"Since when?"

"Yesterday. I mean, last night." She shook her head in frustration. "Fuck! Tonight. What all do you remember happening tonight?"

"Maybe I should be asking you what you remember instead."

She dreaded this kind of response. It made her vulnerable. If nothing had happened between the two of them, then it would be some revealed secret desire, the kind of thing that's revealed from a recluse's stolen diary and broadcast to all those mentioned on its pages. Mortifying and irreparably damaging. So, she doubled down on her unwillingness to answer him, making him reveal first. "Just tell me what's happened, Frank! Don't fucking piss me off with any bullshit!"

She could tell that her tactic worked based on his innocent expression at her threatening words.

"Whoa! Okay. I went into my tent, got my whisky and took a swig. You joined me, and we had whisky. We fell asleep, and I found you out here without your gear and yelling out words that I couldn't make out. I don't think they were English, but they also didn't sound like any language I've ever heard. More like moans or something."

"What? You mean, we didn't . . . " She stopped herself before giving too much away. "So, that's it?"

The end of her question was interrupted by a distinct sound coming from the tree line. It sounded like feet crushing snow. They both turned toward the trees, anticipating something far larger than what emerged from the darkness.

Guin's earlier paralysis from the cold was nothing like the paralysis she experienced now. The figure that emerged from the blackness was her mother, Shirley. Her face glowed in the immense firelight, the rest of her hidden behind clothing and shadows. The woman approached their camp with the look of one under hypnosis, as if the flames served as the metal to her magnetism. And, robotically, she neared the fire, crouched before it, put her hands out in cliché warming fashion, and then plopped down in the snow.

"Mom?" Guin said as the woman got comfortable, but there was no response. "Mom!" she yelled now.

Nothing. She just sat there, warming herself in front of the tall flames.

Her whole purpose for being here was to find something to help shed light on her mother's disappearance, and, now, her mother had shown up out of nowhere, sitting next to the campfire and warming her limbs. Guin didn't know how to respond to this person who was every bit her mother ignoring her as if she was deaf and had no sense of the sounds around her. She just sat there, feet close to the flame, hands outstretched, eyes vacant. She was every bit the interloper at their camp that Guin felt being in this area.

"Mom!" she said again.

Guin wanted to approach her, but she knew that there was something off, something that identified this creature as something that wasn't her mother. An imposter. An interloper. And if none of those things, a woman long since gone from sanity.

It was the first time in Guin's life that she had to question whether to approach her mother. She finally turned her attention to Frank, who stood and watched Shirley as if in a trance. This response by him didn't help clear up her foggy perspective. If anything, it made it worse because she now questioned whether to say anything to make Frank snap out of his trance. His expression mimicked one who was palsied, slack-jawed, and showing the first signs of drool. Guin didn't fully understand what was going on unless it was all part of the same nightmare.

In her periphery, she saw movement from the thing that posed as her mother, so she looked back at it. It was staring at her, eyes a hideous black and head swaying slowly back and forth like a cobra. And then its horrid smile, top and bottom rows of teeth stained and littered with what looked like cooked spinach.

"You're not supposed to be here," the thing said in a voice that was some strange mixture of masculine and feminine. The mouth moved oddly as it said this, as if it was wearing her mother's skin.

"Where am I supposed to be?" she asked without hesitation.

"North," it said, its entire body shaking as if a chill had coasted through its veins. Then, in a frighteningly sharp drop in tone, it said, "You were supposed to stay in the north."

The wildly sharp alterations in tone and the devilish swaying didn't stir Guin. Only those dead eyes stirred her, made her uneasy.

"What are you?" The words left her mouth without getting approval from her brain, and she, again, immediately regretted voicing it. But, another part of her knew that she had done the right thing.

The thing smiled again, and when it replied, stopped swaying. "I am."

Guin didn't understand, and her fears and sadness were overtaken by a need to know, to understand. Like a scientist on the brink of a new discovery, Guin needed to push on and not let any hindering human emotions stand in the way.

"What? You are what?" she yelled.

The thing stood now, never taking its eyes off Guin. Tilting its head to the right, it replied, "We don't have to show ourselves often, but our dormancy and shadow living has unfortunately come to an end."

"I don't—"

"You're not supposed to. And neither are any of the others," it said, glancing at the dazed Frank still looking drugged.

It approached her rapidly, but Guin didn't see its legs moving so it gave the impression that it floated to her like some ghost in a horror film.

"The only thing you need to understand is that you don't belong here, so go home."

Its voice was far more metallic. The stench of its breath like rotting lawn clippings, earthy and pungent. And there was that sting of ozone again, reaching deep in her nostrils and making her eyes water.

Wiping her eyes, she said, "I'm trying."

Now, the thing leaned directly in front of her, and Guin's stomach nearly emptied when she realized that it was indeed wearing her mother's face as a mask, that there was something far more hideous underneath that mask.

"If you stay here another night, I'll do more than just alter your dreams and pull you out of your tent and leave you in the cold." Its tone sharpened now. "If you stay here another night, you'll see your parents again."

When the thing finished threatening her, it leapt with lightning speed, disappearing into the clear night sky, the stars of Gemini, of Castor and Pollux, shimmering as it leapt past them.

Guin just gazed up at those stars, the darkness of space, the vastness. This thing that lived in the wind, this thing that made the stars shift in her sight, it was made up of that stardust as much as she was, it was part of her and she part of it. Maybe that was why she wasn't frightened, why this display hadn't made her scream. And then she finally remembered that Frank had witnessed it all. She turned her attention to him, still standing like a drooling statue at the spot where the thing had been.

"Frank!" she yelled.

Nothing.

"Frank!" she yelled again.

Again, nothing.

Guin marched to the man and shook him until the spell was broken.

"Frank!"

"Yeah," he said.

"Do you have any idea what just happened?"

"No," he said. "I don't even remember coming out here." He glanced down at his boots, then back at Guin. "How long have I been out here?" he asked, a confused expression spread across his cold face.

"What's the last thing you remember?"

"You coming into my tent and taking my CC."

"That's the last thing you remember?"

"It is," he said, giving off the impression that he was someone who often forgot things due to self-medication. And while his was a bit different, the end result was still the same. He didn't remember. He would never truly remember.

Guin just let out a deep breath and lowered her head, whispering to herself, "What the fuck is going on here?"

Crouching now, just a few feet from the fire, Guin tried to balance her mind. If the events from the previous night . . . no, tonight had all been a dream, then was she still dreaming now? Had all of that been her imagination?

"Are you okay?" asked Frank.

She looked up at him with an almost angry expression as she said, "Yes, Frank. It's probably a good idea to just go back into your tent and try to get some sleep. We have a long day tomorrow."

He did as she suggested, leaving her alone with the fire. His willingness to just go back in his tent concerned her. That was not the typical Frank. But nothing seemed to be typical on this terrible night.

Guin breathed in a deep lungful of icy air, closed her eyes, and tried to center herself. It was yet another first for her, this time being unable to distinguish the difference between dream and reality. She let out the air, a warm puff that looked more like she'd just exhaled cigarette smoke than air.

The physical proof, that's what could help determine it, she reasoned. So, she made sure there were tracks where her mother had been. They were indeed there, along with the imprint of her body next to the fire. Since there was no way for her to track where she had gone, Guin would track where she had come from. The tracks came in from the tree line, so she started in that direction and got no more than five steps when something in the darkness peered out at her with menacing yellow eyes like those of a lion. They were in the forest, just beyond the tree line. But they certainly didn't belong to a lion. Not only was it not the correct ecosystem, but the placement was off. These eyes hovered much higher than a lion's would have.

The sight caused her to freeze in her tracks. That all too familiar feeling of paralysis set in again, this time in her legs, as the eyes got closer to the campfire's range. And in a few seconds, she knew what creature held those wild and inhuman eyes. It stepped slowly out of the forest, the great moose, far larger than any moose that roamed these regions. Once in plain view in the shimmering firelight, it stopped and stared at her, its warm breath fogging the view of its face and antlers. The nauseating odor of ozone weakening her demeanor.

She was back to the dream of Max and the great moose. If ever she would understand its meaning, now was the time. Guin was anticipating the beast to explode into a billion snowflakes and engulf her, but that's not what happened. It just stood there, patiently, as if contemplating, each exhalation seeming to emit more dense clouds of visible breath than the previous.

Not really knowing why, she said to the beast, "I'm not Max. I'm not afraid of you."

The beast huffed and began scraping as if to ready itself for a charge.

"I'm still not afraid of you."

It halted its scraping, then stood up onto its hind legs, jolting up and down aggressively the way a goat might do, while bellowing out a strange noise. Not the weird and sometimes comedic grunts and ughs a moose might make, but more like the mixture between a rattlesnake's rattle and a bear's growl. It wasn't until it dropped back down on all fours that Guin approached it rather than letting it come toward her. The great moose watched her with its wild eyes, not flinching, but she sensed that it hadn't expected her to be the aggressor.

With each step closer, Guin felt awe at the creature's size. When she'd seen it at first, it seemed slightly larger than any other moose she'd ever seen, but, now, she realized clearly that it had to be twice the size of the largest moose she'd ever seen. It didn't cause her to slow her pace, just forced her to keep her courage strong. And she kept that courage, not stopping until she was a few feet away from the creature.

It was indeed immense. If she reached up, her hand could grasp the dewlap, that collection of loose skin hanging from its throat. But she didn't reach out, just stood there, head back, staring up at its head. It peered slowly down at her, its yellow eyes seeming to glow in the dark night, the firelight from the campfire giving them a hellish flicker. It was in that moment that she expected the animal to speak to her, to somehow communicate in English what it wanted her to know, but that didn't happen. The moose lowered its head enough for Guin to reach its snout. She knew that it was certainly not a bow in submission, but some primitive form of invitation. It wanted her to touch it.

Instinctively, she took the glove off her right hand and reached out to place it on the beast's snout. Terrible thoughts of it biting down and ripping her hand off or raising itself up on its hind legs to then come crashing down on her with its massive hooves flashed through her mind, but she remained persistent as she had while trudging through the snow toward the thing.

When her hand made contact with the moose, it caused an electric vibration that tensed every muscle in her body. She couldn't pull away, as if her hand to the animal was magnetic. Her eyes closed involuntarily as her body shook. And then it all stopped, her body numb, but she could open her eyes again. As she did so, all senses came back at once, and she found herself above everything, being pulled along by some invisible force as they skirted the treetops at a speed that caused the skin on her cheeks to tighten as it stretched back, stinging from the great force and chill. Had she not worn glasses, she was sure that her eyes would have frozen in their sockets. Below her, the treetops bent as they passed. Above, the stars glowed brilliantly as ever.

Somehow, amid the pain, amid experiencing what could only be described as being part of the wind, Guin had a split-second thought because of those stars above. Each tiny dot was probably responsible for all kinds of life out there, all different kinds of possibilities that the human mind could not even come close to fathoming. How many other places out there had such unknowns as she was experiencing in her own world now? This phenomenon didn't exist in any books, at least not non-fiction books, and, if such esoteric elements were indeed present in her world, then what else was out there? In her world and all the others represented by those flickering dots up in the vast darkness of space? The final element of her brief thought focused solely on her, that she now had firsthand knowledge of something far superior and well hidden, a new member of esoterica, the chosen few that kept arcane knowledge of the world, and kept it from the world, for this information was not for the masses. Religion made it clear that the masses couldn't handle such knowledge.

She stopped abruptly, hovering there above the trees, eyes skyward, limbs wavering as if she were in a pool of water, but there was no water in this aerial baptismal. The invisible priest looked

THE THING IN THE WIND

down on her with its billion yellow eyes, judging her, considering her, and then finally speaking to her. The sound was not external. It seemed to come from within her somehow.

"*You are not ready,*" the voice said.

The sound of the voice reminded Guin of her parents, as if it was their voices combined.

"*You are meant for other things,*" it then said.

"*Release her,*" a different voice said.

At this command, she went into freefall, the multitudinous branches slowing her fall but ripping her gear on the way down until she finally crashed onto the snowy forest floor, bruised and lightly bloodied.

Guin hadn't lost consciousness. When her body plowed into the snow and ground, it knocked the wind out of her. Try as she might to take in air, her body rejected it, like someone under water hoping the gasp they took in would give them replenishing air to only fill their lungs with heavy water, the only difference was that her lungs remained void of anything, so it was weightless. It wasn't until the fourth panicked gasp that her body allowed air in, and she accepted it, repeated it violently, appreciated each icy lungful until her body reset. And it was only a few more gasps after that that her body responded to the subzero temperatures of the forest seeping in through the ragged snow gear that hung from her body.

Guin tried to guess how far from camp she was, but there was no way to tell. She didn't know how fast she'd been pulled by the wind and couldn't even determine what direction the camp was in. It would be another obstacle that she wasn't confident she could surpass. Exhaustion had set in, a deep fatigue that she wasn't familiar with. The only action she could think to take was to somehow get a fire going, but that seemed fruitless because everything was covered in snow. Trying to ignite anything at such temperatures and dampness would give the same result as trying to light an ice cube on fire.

There was one thing she could do . . . hope! She could let her instinct guide her and hope that it would take her in the right direction. Part of that hope was Frank. If she called out his name, maybe he'd hear her and help guide her back to camp. After everything that had happened, there couldn't be a downside to this strategy, so she did it.

"Frank!" she screamed. "Fraaaaannnnk!"

Nothing.

She didn't bother continuing screaming, just started trudging through the snowy forest in the direction that felt right. And she kept going for nearly an hour. There was no sign of campfire through sight or smell, but she could only rely on her instincts, so she kept moving forward. It was at that moment that she heard the grumbling somewhere in the blackness. This grumbling was a sound she knew and was all too familiar with. There was a bear nearby. While it should have begun its hibernation, the recent events didn't hold any norms as norms any longer.

Guin slowed her pace, kept eying everything around her every other step, and tried to get a true determination of which direction the bear was in. It didn't help that snow had begun to fall, the once clear and transparent night now cloud-covered. With each loud, squeaky, and crunchy step through the snow, Guin tensed, tried to focus her energy on her sense of sound to determine if the bear had heard her. And when she didn't hear the grumbling or heavy breathing after several steps, part of her wondered if she'd imagined it all, but the discussion earlier about many hunters being absent this bear season made her confidence in that idea waver, so much so that she broke safety advice and started running, hoping to get out of any potential range of a hungry bear. That was the last challenge she needed tonight, already having dealt with dream love and what most would consider to be a supernatural experience. Not to mention a probable concussion from the fall. All she wanted now was to get back to the camp and get the hell out of the Black Lake region.

Her energy hit empty after only a few minutes, and she dropped to her knees, her breathing labored and her confidence minimal. It wasn't some obscure element of Nature that would take her down, it'd just be simple temperature. While she had been pushing herself to cover as much ground as possible, keeping her body temperature up, reality hit her when her body just couldn't keep going. The cold settled in so quickly, seeming to sense her exhaustion and readying itself for the death blow.

But, Guin was a fighter. She sensed this, and that gave her the last sliver of energy to push on for a few minutes longer, like an engine without oil, before allowing her body to collapse into the snow and let Mother Nature work her over.

Like a personal trainer that knew their subject more than they knew themselves, Guin gave it that last push. When she had reached her true point of exhaustion that no amount of will could have reignited, that's when she heard a response to her original call. Frank had come for her, but she had no energy to respond. Even if she had the energy, she was so dehydrated that the sound wouldn't have traveled more than a light whisper.

Guin lay there, eyes skyward. Too exhausted to speak or move, she was at Frank's mercy, at Frank's ability to find what he was looking for. As her eyelids grew heavier, she could hear the crunching sound of mashing snow get louder.

"Guin! Please tell me you're alive!"

Her eyes were barely open, and she tilted her head in his direction. That was all the answer he would get.

"I'm going to get you out of here, Guin. Camp's not far."

And he dragged her there, silently, the whole ordeal lasting no more than fifteen minutes. She thanked her instincts and any other element that had helped guide her in the right direction. Those instincts had gotten her back to her camp.

Frank laid her down inside his tent.

"There's blood on your face. Tell me where else you're hurt."

Guin shook her head. Her whole body was in some form of pain, but the only blood that had been spilled was from her exposed skin.

Letting out a sigh of relief, Frank said, "Thank goodness." He then zipped the doors together, locked them with a zip tie, and lay down beside her. "We just have to last the rest of the night, and we're out of here in the morning," he said. "I'll make sure of that."

Guin lay there, hearing but not responding, feeling him as he put his arm around her and held her close to him, making sure her body was able to warm up. She soon heard his light snoring. She listened to it for several hours until the tent began to lighten, letting her know that a new day had actually begun and that the ominous but enlightening night was finally over.

ix

The sun made her feel safe, and she exited the tent and got the morning fire started. Had the night lasted even an hour longer, it would have driven her crazy. The thoughts. The terrible thoughts. But, it wasn't what had actually happened to her last night, it was the uncertainty of what had been real and what had been dream. This most recent bout of insomnia didn't help matters, so she turned to keeping busy by getting the fire going and filling her belly with warm coffee strong enough to kill those who had not spent days in the wilderness fending off the elements both natural and seemingly supernatural.

Frank did not stir for another hour. In that time, Guin had sipped through three cups of coffee and changed out her ripped outerwear with two sweaters and an extra pair of long underwear. It would make the trek more difficult, much colder, but she had no other choice. As long as it didn't snow, she could stay dry. As long as the wind didn't pick up too much, she could stay warm enough.

When Frank did emerge from the tent, Guin said, "Should probably make quick work of breakfast and packing up. We've got a long day ahead of us."

"Sure," he said.

It was clear that Frank didn't fully grasp the events from the previous night, or since they stepped foot in Stony Rapids. The man's brother was gone. Two others were gone. She had almost been added to that list, but Frank had searched for her and saved her. None of that appeared to have been remembered based on his expression and the sound of his voice, but maybe he was just being strong for her. Even with such forces at work, she didn't believe Frank would not remember his brother being taken.

Guin needed to be sure, so she asked, "Do you know what's going on, Frank?"

"Breakfast?" he blurted out. "I'm starving." He then proceeded to take the last slices of bread and make himself a chicken sandwich with the canned meat he'd brought.

It just didn't make sense, she thought.

"Frank," she said sternly. "What do you think happened yesterday? Specifically, last night?"

He took a bite of his sandwich, shaking his head, then saying with food in his mouth, "Well, we finished my bottle of CC." He swallowed, but it took a few tries to get all the food down. "Then I was out."

Guin just stared at him, not really knowing what kind of expression was drawn across her face, but his response made it clear that it wasn't pleasant.

"I feel like I'm missing something here."

THE THING IN THE WIND

It was like déjà vu. But, she played along. "So, you don't remember anything after starting to drink your whisky?"

"You're making me feel like I did something terrible," he said more seriously now. "Is there something—"

"Nothing like that, Frank," she said reassuringly. "What about your brother? Do you remember—"

"Fuck," he said, dropping his breakfast into the snow, his expression shifting to one that aged him ten years. "We've gotta get outta here."

Whatever spell he had been under that had been clouding his memory suddenly lost its power over him, at least most of it based on his change in demeanor.

Guin had a sudden sense of superiority. Not only could she remember all that had happened, but she now had a deeper knowledge of the universe and what lies beyond one of its many veils. And, second, whatever had afflicted Frank made it clearer why so many didn't know about the thing lurking in this region. Those who had come in contact with it, they must have been put under some kind of spell, making the memories fuzzy or non-existent. The idea of this kind of power made Guin shudder. Not only did she possess this firsthand knowledge, minuscule as it may be, but she also understood the possibility of other mythologies being based in reality. All those tales spanning back to ancient times, had they all been true? A creature in Loch Ness? La Llorona in Mexico? Krakens in the sea? Or, even Cerberus standing guard at the gates of the Underworld? At least to some extent? And, somehow, she and few others had immunity to the power of those creatures, had escaped, and had returned to tell the tales.

X

The morning remained sunny with temperatures just below freezing. Guin's legs ached something terrible. All of the stress, fatigue, and bruises seemed to have waited until now to hit her at once, not to mention a light nausea from not sleeping. She didn't allow it to slow her pace, knowing that they had to reach Stony Rapids before dusk, so she trudged on, feeling as though she was carrying an extra hundred pounds on her shoulders, even though she'd left behind most of her provisions and tent.

The heavier weight was in her mind. Her parents were gone,

but at least she had enough answers for that to be able to move on. What nagged at her, though, what caused her immense frustration was not knowing the significance of the dream. It had started decades ago with her mother. And it wasn't even the need for an explanation as to why *she* had had the dream, for she knew that a clear explanation could have been the influence from her mother's journals. Guin needed the explanation for the dream's beginning, why her mother had had it night after night. And what significance it may have played in what had happened here. The only connections that she was able to make were hypothesizing that the frozen river had been the clearing from the dream and that there was a chance that the cabin they'd come across was where Max the boy used to live, but there was nothing concrete, or even remotely concrete for that matter, to lead her to believe it was part of the dream. Guin wasn't even sure if this place had anything to do with it at all. It could have just been a dream, some story her mind conjured up, maybe influenced by something Shirley had watched or read. But, if that had been the case, then why was it bothering her now? Why hadn't it settled like the other elements? Why did it feel like it was a significant part of that weight on her shoulders?

These and similar questions swirled as the hours passed. By mid-afternoon, Frank saw a structure, and then another one.

"I think we made it," he said, pointing ahead. "I think those are the houses we passed at the end of Stony Rapids."

Guin saw them clearly, but it didn't give her a sense of relief.

"Looks like everyone's still gone, though," he added.

Frank picked up his pace, then stopped abruptly when Guin blurted out, "Frank, tell me again Miksa's story."

She noticed that her voice had startled him, and he looked back at her, waiting for her to catch up.

"Do you want to get to the boat—"

"I don't."

"Okay. What do you want to know?"

"I'm not sure. You said that his father died when he was eight and his journey to the village left him frostbitten."

"Yeah."

"How long ago did that actually happen?"

Frank pondered this for a moment. "I'm pretty sure it had to be the early 1980s. If I recall, Miksa got to town, and it was a thriving area across the northern stretch of the lake. Uranium City.

Hell, even Camsell had more than a hundred times the people there are now. All of that changed in 1982 when the mines closed, so, yeah, sometime around then."

It hit her like an avalanche, nearly shoving her down to the damp snow. Finally, there was a potential connection. That Miksa's brush with the elements coincided with her mother's dream about Max.

"And you never really spoke to him?"

Shaking his head, he said, "No, that was all Berin." He huffed, then added, "He didn't talk about him much either. Spent hours talking to him and barely offered a sentence or two to me about it. I didn't pry either. Figured he was working through the Julia stuff."

Guin nodded in response, then started moving forward again. She knew that the only place to get answers was the horse's mouth, so she'd do just that once they got back on the boat.

But, first, they'd have to report the others missing to the RCMP. As they passed the intersection with 964, they slogged forward another few hundred yards before finding themselves in front of the RCMP post. The front door was unlocked, both 4×4s and both snowmobiles parked out front, but there was no one inside.

"Hello!" yelled Frank.

The only reply was the wind.

"Hello!" he yelled again, this time much louder.

Still nothing.

"Use your radio and see if it goes through," said Guin.

Frank pulled the walkie-talkie from his pack, turned it on, and said, "Testing, testing, testing."

The sound came through on the RCMP channel loud and clear.

"They either left between the time we headed out and now or something's happened here," Frank said.

"I think we need to go to the boat right now, Frank. Miksa wasn't picking up earlier, so we should see if he's still there."

Frank didn't respond, just made for the exit, Guin following close behind. The trawler was there, tied to the dock, so they approached rapidly. When they reached the fence, Guin noticed that the little shrike had been busy, having added what had to be twenty mice to the barbs.

"Like Vlad the Impaler," she said to herself.

"Miksa!" yelled Frank.

The aroma of cooking fish grew stronger as they approached the vessel and boarded.

"Miksa!" Frank yelled again.

"Below," came a ragged and weak reply.

Shedding their packs, Frank and Guin got themselves below deck. The table was covered in bones. Fish bones. It was as if Miksa had started eating when they left and hadn't stopped until this moment. But, to look at the man, it was as if he hadn't had a bite to eat in weeks. His skin seemed to hang just a bit looser over his bones, eyes sunken in.

"Miksa. I'm glad you're okay. Have you had the radio with you the whole time?"

"I have," he said, pointing to his chest. It hung there around a rope he wore around his neck. "Nothing's come through since you left, but I knew nothing would come through."

"What?"

"As did your brother, but he insisted."

"What are you talking about?"

"Did you know what was going to happen?" Guin said with anger, teeth clenching.

"Not like you might think." He motioned to the table. "Let's sit, please. Berin asked me to talk to you when you returned. I think it's why he wanted me along in the first place."

They sat.

"Go on," Frank said.

"I had no premonitions or anything like that." Miksa's tired gaze met Frank's. "Your brother and I spoke at length, at great length about Julia. And," he said, turning his attention to Guin, "when your father hired him, something changed in Berin." He let out a labored breath, his attention shifting to the bones on the table. "I don't know if your brother told you anything about our conversations, but you're probably aware of how I came to live in Camsell Portage. The incident at my father's cabin when I was eight."

"I know a little."

"Well, there were a few details that I kept from him. Not on purpose or anything, I had just forgotten. Meaningless details. But, when he came over and told me that he was making one final push to find out what happened to Julia, it happened. The wind picked up, and it carried with it an odor that I hadn't smelled since I was eight. I don't really know how to describe it, but it was strong, bitter—"

"Like ozone," Guin said, noticing Miksa break his stare at the bones and meet her eyes. "It smelled like ozone." She barely got the last word out as a knot had secretly formed in her throat and choked her. She clenched her teeth again, holding back tears. This detail disturbed her the most. She realized that whatever he had come across was the same or like the same thing that they'd come into contact with out there.

"Okay, ozone," he agreed. "The scent took me back to that terrible experience in the woods that made me like this." He raised his hand which was missing three fingers. "And, in my gut, I knew that if he went out there, he would have a similar fate."

"What did happen to you when you were eight?" Guin asked, her voice deep as if she had a cold.

Miksa closed his eyes and shook his head.

"*Tell us*," she insisted.

"I got lost. I was out of food, so I had to get to town, but my only means was on foot. There was a lot of snow, and I didn't know the way."

"I don't buy it," Guin said.

"Guin," Frank interjected. "That's what Berin told me."

"I think you need to tell us what really happened," she said with a lowered brow, eyes piercing.

Miksa was silent for what felt like ten minutes before letting out a deep breath and asking, "How do you—"

"You weren't going out for food," she said sternly. "Something called you. Something made you leave your warm bed. You didn't really want to leave the warmth, so you stalled when you reached the fire, but your attention turned to your strange reflections in the warped glass of the front door. And the eyes of the moose head above the fire." She saw Miksa's mouth widening at her description of her mother's dream. "And then you went out into that windy and snowy night, running through the trees, until you reached the clearing. And you saw it. The great moose."

She saw Miksa mouth the words *great moose* as she spoke them.

"How did you know about that?"

"And then it shifted, bursting into a snowy gale and taking you into the sky. To the stars."

There were tears forming in Miksa's eyes now, old and wrinkled chin quivering.

"But the name it called you was not Miksa. It was—"

"Max," he said in a loud and pained whisper, closing his eyes and bowing his head and struggling to swallow.

"Max," she said, tears now staining her cheeks. So, it was true. The dream had been real. Her mother had some kind of connection with this man and his encounter with whatever that thing in the forest had been.

"Why Max?" asked Frank. "I don't understand the name difference."

"My family is rooted in Hungary and the Czech Republic. My first name is Maximilian. Everyone but my father called me Max. He called me Miksa, so I honor him by keeping it." Through more tears, Miksa forced out, "But how do you know this?"

"Do you know anything about my mother, Shirley Wells?"

"I'm sorry, I don't," he said, shaking his head.

There had to be something. There was no way that she and her mother had recurring dreams about this man's horrific experience without there being some kind of connection. Maybe that was it. Recurring.

"Do you ever have recurring dreams?"

He thought about it, sitting there with his forehead wrinkled in a concerned way, trying his best to collect himself at these revelations and stifle his tears so that he could think more clearly. It took a few moments, and then he remembered. "I used to," Miksa replied. "Yes, a few days after I somehow showed up in Fond du Lac, I recall something about a girl and a tree. I don't know what kind of tree, but it was large. Massive. It was a strange dream. It wasn't fluid, more like images from a View-Master. You know, those toys with the picture reels. Looks like binoculars. It was like that. I remember a girl standing in front of a tree with a book, then sitting against the tree reading the book, then looking on in horror at construction machinery, then standing in front of a gravestone. That would replay multiple times each night for a couple years, then it stopped."

All were silent when Miksa finished.

Guin understood now. It actually made sense, to a degree. While she didn't believe in things that were required for it to fully make sense, like kindred spirits and other supernatural elements, it was an explanation that she could live with. Miksa didn't have any further answers for her. For her to move on, she had to accept what this revealed to her. Miksa held arcane knowledge and had wanted to escape, and he did so with plenty of battle wounds. Her mother had escaped the shackles of Tennessee, yearning for that deep-rooted connection to Nature, found it, and became part of it, not wanting to escape the way Miksa had. As for Guin, she hadn't so much escaped as, for some reason, Nature had her in its grasp and let her go, leaving her as a beacon of arcane knowledge and understanding. She could only assume that a similar scenario had fit Berin and Julia's fate. As for Annalisa and Edmund, that would just have to remain a mystery. Had she known them, it might have caused further research, but they had been strangers to her. She had to draw the line somewhere if she was going to be able to move on, so she did. The line was firm, and she refused to approach it again.

"Thank you, Miksa." Turning to Frank, she said, "Can we go home now?"

Her words were not met with a response yet. She understood that Frank may not have gotten all the answers he needed to move on, but was he her concern? No. But, that sliver of empathy that dwelled within her agreed to try. And what she said next was not easy for her.

Placing her gloved hand on his, she said, "He's with his Julia now, Frank, as my father is with my mother. Let's be content with that."

Frank turned to her, the skin on his face seeming to have aged a decade since reaching the boat. Taking in and then exhaling a deep breath, he then said while nodding, "I think we have to."

She nodded. "Will you stay in Camsell?"

Staring at the floor, he said in a monotone voice, "No." His word seemed to snap him out of his morbid staring. He looked at her. "I think it's time I go somewhere new."

Guin didn't know if he was implying that he follow her up north, even if she was a married woman, but it did incite certain thoughts. What was she going to do once she got back to Yellowknife? While she had only kissed another man, the sexual encounter had been a dream after all, it was clear that she had to cut ties with Jacob. Even though the man loved her with every ounce of his body and soul, he just didn't fit. She thrived in the north while he dwindled, so that would be the first decision when she got back. And, if Frank was implying that he should follow her, she was not okay with that either. While he certainly fit more snugly than Jacob, Guin knew that the only companion she needed and desired was the north. She had to shed her skin, cut all ties, and approach the north freely and clearly, not letting anything get in the way. Mostly, she yearned for her lake, to stroll out on the dock, lean on the rail, and open up to it, let it know her secrets, and understand her wants and desires. And, maybe, after all of this, it meant that her lake would feed her its secrets as well.

So, to be sure, she followed up with, "And where do you need to go?"

Frank looked to Miksa when he asked, "What part of Hungary is that side of your family from?"

Miksa said, "Ercsi, just south of Budapest along the Danube."

"I think we'll go to Ercsi, just south of Budapest along the Danube."

The response brought a smile to all three.

"And you?" Frank asked.

She glanced down, smiled, then looked deeply into Frank's eyes. "I belong to the north. So, if you ever need to find me, I'll be in Yellowknife."

He nodded, fully understanding what she meant.

"We should get going," Frank said.

With that, the three of them prepared to disembark, taking the trawler back across Lake Athabasca, the mysterious Lake of the Hills, to Fort Chipewyan. From there, Frank and Miksa would make preparations to visit Miksa's homeland back in Hungary. Guin, a new keeper of mystical and arcane knowledge, would begin her short journey back to the icy, secluded capital of the north.

THE END?

Not if you want to dive into more of Crystal Lake Publishing's Tales from the Darkest Depths!

Check out our amazing website and online store
or download our latest catalog here.
https://geni.us/CLPCatalog

Looking for award-winning Dark Fiction?
Download our latest catalog.

Includes our anthologies, novels, novellas, collections,
poetry, non-fiction, and specialty projects.

WHERE STORIES COME ALIVE!

We always have great new projects and content on the website to dive into, as well as a newsletter, behind the scenes options, social media platforms, our own dark fiction shared-world series and our very own webstore. Our webstore even has categories specifically for KU books, non fiction, anthologies, and of course more novels and novellas.

ABOUT THE AUTHOR

Bill Mullen was born in England and holds an MFA from the Bluegrass Writers Studio. He now lives in Kentucky where he teaches literature and writing at Eastern Kentucky University. His first novel, *Red Nocturne*, was published in 2016.

Readers . . .

Thank you for reading *The Thing in the Wind*. We hope you enjoyed this novel.

If you have a moment, please review *The Thing in the Wind* at the store where you bought it.

Help other readers by telling them why you enjoyed this book. No need to write an in-depth discussion. Even a single sentence will be greatly appreciated. Reviews go a long way to helping a book sell, and is great for an author's career. It'll also help us to continue publishing quality books.

Thank you again for taking the time to journey with Crystal Lake Publishing.

Visit our Linktree page for a list of our social media platforms. https://linktr.ee/CrystalLakePublishing

Follow us on Amazon:

MISSION STATEMENT:

Since its founding in August 2012, Crystal Lake Publishing has quickly become one of the world's leading publishers of Dark Fiction and Horror books. In 2023, Crystal Lake Publishing formed a part of Crystal Lake Entertainment, joining several other divisions, including Torrid Waters, Crystal Lake Comics, Crystal Lake Kids, and many more.

While we strive to present only the highest quality fiction and entertainment, we also endeavour to support authors along their writing journey. We offer our time and experience in non-fiction projects, as well as author mentoring and services, at competitive prices.

With several Bram Stoker Award wins and many other wins and nominations (including the HWA's Specialty Press Award), Crystal Lake Publishing puts integrity, honor, and respect at the forefront of our publishing operations.

We strive for each book and outreach program we spearhead to not only entertain and touch or comment on issues that affect our readers, but also to strengthen and support the Dark Fiction field and its authors.

Not only do we find and publish authors we believe are destined for greatness, but we strive to work with men and women who endeavour to be decent human beings who care more for others than themselves, while still being hard working, driven, and passionate artists and storytellers.

Crystal Lake Publishing is and will always be a beacon of what passion and dedication, combined with overwhelming teamwork and respect, can accomplish. We endeavour to know each and every one of our readers, while building personal relationships with our authors, reviewers, bloggers, podcasters, bookstores, and libraries.

We will be as trustworthy, forthright, and transparent as any business can be, while also keeping most of the headaches away from our authors, since it's our job to solve the problems so they can stay in a creative mind. Which of course also means paying our authors.

We do not just publish books, we present to you worlds within your world, doors within your mind, from talented authors who sacrifice so much for a moment of your time.

There are some amazing small presses out there, and through collaboration and open forums we will continue to support other presses in the goal of helping authors and showing the world what quality small presses are capable of accomplishing. No one wins when a small press goes down, so we will always be there to support hardworking, legitimate presses and their authors. We don't see Crystal Lake as the best press out there, but we will always strive to be the best, strive to be the most interactive and grateful, and even blessed press around. No matter what happens over time, we will also take our mission very seriously while appreciating where we are and enjoying the journey.

What do we offer our authors that they can't do for themselves through self-publishing?

We are big supporters of self-publishing (especially hybrid publishing), if done with care, patience, and planning. However, not every author has the time or inclination to do market research, advertise, and set up book launch strategies. Although a lot of authors are successful in doing it all, strong small presses will always be there for the authors who just want to do what they do best: write.

What we offer is experience, industry knowledge, contacts and trust built up over years. And due to our strong brand and trusting fanbase, every Crystal Lake Publishing book comes with weight of respect. In time our fans begin to trust our judgment and will try a new author purely based on our support of said author.

With each launch we strive to fine-tune our approach, learn from our mistakes, and increase our reach. We continue to assure our authors that we're here for them and that we'll carry the weight of the launch and dealing with third parties while they focus on their strengths—be it writing, interviews, blogs, signings, etc.

We also offer several mentoring packages to authors that include knowledge and skills they can use in both traditional and self-publishing endeavours.

We look forward to launching many new careers.

This is what we believe in. What we stand for. This will be our legacy.

Welcome to Crystal Lake Publishing— Tales from the Darkest Depths.

Printed in Great Britain
by Amazon

40938839R00099